S........IN
OCC............ECTIVE

CAREFUL WHAT
YOU WISH FOR

BRON JAMES

First published in 2020
Copyright © 2020 Bron James
ISBN 979-8-687-61527-3

~

www.bronjames.co.uk
www.samhainscasebook.co.uk

SAM HAIN
CAREFUL WHAT YOU WISH FOR

PROLOGUE

If there was one thing Deirdre Roberts could never have imagined, it was the drastic and inexplicable turn her life was about to take. Nor could she possibly have believed that the fickle threads of fate were to hinge upon a seemingly inconsequential visit to a nondescript little antique shop in Islington.

It had all started two weeks ago, on an otherwise unremarkable Sunday afternoon.

Deirdre awoke early that morning. She ironed her Sunday-best, put curlers in her hair, and set about preparing breakfast, all the while doing her utmost not to accidentally wake her husband. Cedric was not much of a morning person, and he was prone to be stuck in an irritable mood for the rest of the day should he be woken before his alarm clock. Deirdre, by comparison, would often be up with the sunrise; especially to get ready for church on Sundays. After almost forty years of marriage, and several arguments about what precisely was the proper time to start a day, she and Cedric were very unlikely to change their habits, but they had settled into their own routine and rhythm.

The day had proceeded at a fairly predictable

pace. Once Cedric had woken up, they both sat down to enjoy a breakfast of lightly boiled eggs and heavily buttered toast, before Deirdre left for church. Following the Sunday service, she and some of the other women from the congregation had decided to go for afternoon tea together. She and her friends shared stories of their children and grandchildren, gossiped about the goings-on of almost every soap opera on TV that past week, and talked about Ingrid's new tablecloths, while eating little cucumber sandwiches and miniature sponge cakes.

Knowing that their husbands were contently down the pub or at home – probably watching the football or enjoying an early afternoon doze, in either case – they had taken to wandering around the shops of Islington. They idly ventured along the high street, casually window-shopping as they passed the parade of shops, occasionally stopping to browse for new clothes or books. It was in one shop – a relatively hidden little store just off of the high street, somewhere along a quaint-looking passage – that Deirdre found herself perusing antiques.

She had always had a passion for antiquing. She would often frequent markets, antique stores and second-hand shops, searching for hidden treasures. There was nothing she enjoyed more than the thrill of finding a stunning piece of furniture, a beautiful work of art or simply an interesting trinket to display. It had been a while since she had last been antiquing, though; the last time was a while ago in Hampstead, when she'd been knocked over and into a display of china cups by two men in well-tailored suits chasing another man through the market. She had needed a hip operation after that incident. But now she was relishing delving into a world of the aesthetically antique again, and discovering what charming curiosities it had to offer.

The shop looked as if it belonged to an eccentric Victorian hoarder. Every inch of the space was taken up with a clutter of antiquities. The walls were decorated with various pictures and portraits, grainy photographs and artfully illustrated maps. Countless pieces of old wooden furniture, from intricately carved cabinets and dressing-tables to ornate shelves and ostentatious armchairs, formed angular aisles through the small store. Each surface was adorned with all manner of ornaments and mirrors, sets of crockery and cutlery, and myriad unusual objects from bygone eras. Even the floor was covered in the shop's wares, lined with rows of aged Persian rugs.

For Deirdre, this was an absolute haven.

There was one thing in particular amongst this immense treasure trove which had caught her eye. It was a curiously shaped metal vase. At a distance it appeared to be almost golden, even though its surface was marred with aged marks and the tarnish of time. It sat atop a chest of drawers, standing out amidst a collection of jewellery boxes and candleholders. Its base was wide and bulbous, curving up and inward into a tall and narrow stem, before opening up into a large-lipped rim. A cap sealed the top of the vase. Even though the thing was evidently old, the metal having lost some of its sheen and its patterns partially obscured by signs of wear, it still seemed to gleam beneath the orange lights.

As she passed the vase, Deirdre paused to take a closer look. It was cast from iron and almost completely adorned with gilt detailing, the signs of wear being from the metal rusting between the golden patterns. She examined it, delicately tracing her fingers across the design. It was intricate and ornamented, although much of it she couldn't quite make out. The dense collection of patterns twisted and weaved around the bulbous base, with peculiar symbols etched along the sides of the long neck. A nine-pointed star, and several more strange symbols, adorned the cap.

Inquisitively, she gave the lid of the vase a cursory twist and a pull, but it refused to budge. Presumably age had long since sealed it shut, the metal stiff and uncompromising. In some ways, Deirdre knew how it felt. *But maybe with a little bit of polish, a bit of a clean up*, she thought, *this would look quite nice on the mantelpiece.* She turned the vase over in her hands. *If I can get the cap off, too, it would look lovely holding some magnolia blossoms.* Before she had even finished her thought, Deirdre was already at the counter of the antique shop, handing her debit card to the woman behind the till.

That evening, as the sun was setting and Cedric was pulling up weeds in the back garden, Deirdre sat on the patio, hunched over in a garden chair, armed with a cloth and a bottle of polish. She had been scrubbing at the vase, vigorously polishing and gradually cleaning away the marks of age and traces of rust. More and more, the golden patterns were becoming clearer and more distinct, and began to shine and gleam in the evening sun. Aside from a few patches where the metal had been irreparably worn down, it was almost looking as good as new. All that remained was the rigid cap which so stubbornly sealed the vase shut.

'- so Brian had his money on Millwall, of all people,' Cedric carried on relaying the events of his day. He had been talking about the football for what had felt like an eternity to Deirdre. She occasionally nodded her head or made a "mhm" or "ah" sound to feign interest, but beyond this the conversation had been decidedly one-sided. 'Of course, by the second half he was a laughing stock,' he continued, undeterred that he was the only one talking. He had yet to ask her about the vase, if he'd even noticed it at all.

'Ced,' Deirdre eventually spoke with a weary sigh. She held the neck of the vase in a firm grip, and was trying to twist the cap free. 'I love you dearly, but I do wish you would shut up. I could use a hand here with-' There was a creaking groan followed by a pop as the cap was pulled loose, and there seemed to be a sudden rush of air. It almost sounded as if the wind was whistling over the lip of the vase. She beamed triumphantly at her husband. 'Ah, all it needed was a little elbow grease,' she declared. 'This'll look lovely on the mantelpiece, don't you think? Maybe a few flowers?'

Cedric didn't answer. He simply looked at her,

then at the vase, and nodded with an approving smile, and turned his attention back to the weeds poking their heads up amongst the hydrangeas.

The atmosphere at the dinner table that night was a tense and frosty one. Deirdre had prepared a light evening meal for she and Cedric, but when she had dished up their dinner and placed a plate in front of her husband, he did not say a word. No "thank you," not even a sound to acknowledge her. She decided to let it slide, for the moment; they hadn't got through four decades without giving each other a bit of patience. Even if she did find his attitude to be grating at times.

'How's the fish, Ced?' she asked, after an unwelcome and unnaturally awkward stretch of silence. Cedric still did not speak. He delicately cut at the fish fillet, taking a mouthful, and began to quietly chew. The sound of the cutlery clanking and scraping across the crockery was almost deafening against the silence. Dropping her knife and fork onto her plate with a clatter, Deirdre leaned imploringly across the table towards her husband. 'What's wrong, dear? You haven't breathed a word all evening.'

Cedric remained silent. He paused, slowly lowering his cutlery to the plate, and stared at her. His eyes met his wife's gaze, looking at him with a concerned and curious expression. For a moment, it seemed as if he was about to say something, but instead he picked up his cutlery and resumed silently eating.

Slapping her hands against the tabletop, causing their plates and cutlery to bounce, Deirdre pressed herself up from her seat. 'Oh for heaven's sake,' she exclaimed, exasperated, 'I've had enough of this childish behaviour, I really have. Whatever it is that's bothering you, we're not going to get anywhere with this pointless silent treatment.'

Her husband stared up at her, looking like a deer caught in the headlights. His mouth opened, but no words came out.

'Nothing to say for yourself?' she asked – no, she *demanded* – but still Cedric did not utter a word. 'Honestly,' Deirdre huffed, and stormed out of the room. As she began to ascend the stairs, her voice came drifting back down into the dining room. 'You can wash up. I'm going to bed. And you better buck up your ideas by tomorrow, Cedric.'

CHAPTER I

The little rusted bell above the entrance softly tinkled as the door was pushed open, and Alice Carroll stepped through into her new workplace. Her nose twitched and wrinkled as the smell of dust, aged wood, and the faint hint of polish immediately greeted her. She had only been working in the shop for a week and, although she had started to settle into the role, the persistently musty atmosphere would take some getting used to.

It had been quite by coincidence (not that there ever truly is such a thing) that she discovered this job vacancy, glimpsing it in passing shortly before she got wrapped up in another arcane adventure with Sam Hain. And what a happy coincidence it had been. The shop was only a short walk from her flat, which made for a far nicer and more relaxed commute into work than the usual tube journey. The work was relatively laid-back, the pay was decent, and the hours were – within reason – quite flexible.

The owner, Fran Hendricks, was a formidably officious old woman on first impressions, but once one got to know her a little better she was in fact quite sweet. All in all, Alice was enjoying her new job. Plus, the place hadn't been tainted by some terrible supernatural force or inexplicably horrifying event. *Yet*, she thought, patting the top of a wooden cabinet as she passed.

Shuffling off her denim jacket, Alice draped it over the hook of a tall Victorian coat stand, and paused briefly to fix her hair in the ornate mirror which hung on the wall next to it. She began to make her way through the rows of antique furniture which formed the aisles of the store, adjusting a couple of the ornaments on top of a dresser as she passed, and chimed the service bell on the counter. 'Misses Hendricks,' she called out towards the open doorway to the room at the back of the shop, 'I'm here.'

'Oh hello, Alice, dear,' replied an old voice, which creaked like a particularly cheery floorboard. 'How are you?'

'I'm fine, thanks,' Alice said, 'and you?'

The clinking of crockery tinkered from the back room, and a moment later a short, elderly woman emerged. Fran Hendricks was a stern looking woman approaching her mid-seventies. Piercing blue eyes stared out from beneath a perpetually furrowed brow, as if she was always fiercely examining everything she looked at. A beak-like nose hooked over a downward turned mouth, her features exaggerated by the many creases and folds which lined her face. But, despite her harsh appearances, her face softened into a kindly smile as she saw Alice.

'Oh I'm all right, thanks, dear,' she said. 'We've

had some new things come in this morning. Some of it's a load of old tat, but someone's bound to buy it. No accounting for taste...' She paused, gesturing dismissively towards a cabinet in the far corner. 'Got a nice nineteen-forties china tea set, though. If I didn't have a business to run, I'd keep it myself.' She chuckled, and began to walk Alice through the new items.

The tea set was, indeed, quite nice. It was made of fine bone china, all decorated in discreet, pastel-coloured floral patterns. There were some minor signs of age, a hairline crack or two, but overall they had been kept in remarkable condition. On the shelf below, a small army of Toby jugs had mustered together, their grotesque faces leering with soulless eyes at Alice. These were decidedly less appealing, and reminded Alice of a similar hideous collection of nightmarish jugs her grandmother had once had. The things had always disturbed her as a child, whenever she had stayed at her grandparents' house. Even as an adult, their faces inspired something not too dissimilar to a fight-or-flight response in her.

A collection of ornate brass candlesticks were arranged on top of one of the old wooden dressers. They were intricately crafted, the metalwork boasting the embellishments of an art nouveau style, and had been priced at a shockingly high value. Rare originals, Fran had explained, in practically pristine condition despite being older than herself and Alice combined.

While they walked about the store, a couple of customers had come in to browse. Fran and Alice had greeted them cordially and left them to peruse the items at their leisure, although Fran's explanations of the new stock became louder and more exuberant, attempting to draw the attention of the customers. It slowly began to resemble a small guided tour of antiquities, while Fran effused her admiration and love for each exquisite item.

After some time, Alice soon found herself back behind the till. She had been helping a customer with some of the more obscure ornaments, and was ringing through an astrolabe. They were among some of her favourite items in the shop, she had told the man as she neatly wrapped it in tissue paper. Astrolabes, as well as the array of pocket watches, compasses and sextants too. She had discovered she was quite fond of the strange and intricate mechanisms, although she couldn't think of a practical use for them in her day-to-day life. It was a very rare occurrence she found herself out at sea, she considered, and an even rarer one that she would require a sextant to navigate. She wasn't even sure what an astrolabe would be used for. Practicality wasn't the point, though; they would make for cool decorative pieces nonetheless.

'Alright, Alice, love,' Fran's voice creaked, 'I'm going to head out for lunch. You okay to hold the fort while I'm out?'

Alice nodded. 'Of course.' She looked around the quiet store. A man stood in the corner considering the rolls of Moroccan rugs, but other than him, Fran and Alice, there was no one else in the shop. It rarely was an overly busy place. 'I'm sure I can manage.'

'Jolly good,' Fran replied, 'I'll be about an hour or two, I've got to meet someone about an oak cabinet.' She picked up her handbag, fussed over the arrangement of nesting dolls on the counter, and shuffled her way towards the door. Although it could not be said that Fran Hendricks ever moved as if she was in a rush to be anywhere, she walked with considerable purpose out of the shop and along the alley, until she was out of sight.

The next half an hour passed by with little consequence. The man who had been browsing the rugs had left shortly after, and someone else had come in to buy a mantel clock, but other than that not much else had happened. Alice had paced around the shop, fiddling with the displays and adjusting them ever so slightly, to keep herself busy. She polished the glass fronts, and dusted off the tops of the cabinets which Fran always had difficulty reaching. She had to do something to make her feel like she was earning her keep, at least. It wasn't long until she had exhausted her options, though, and after a while she found herself scrolling through her phone in the times between customers.

She had downloaded an ebook on witchcraft the other night after falling down an internet rabbit hole, taking her from a forum sharing ghost stories to websites on the occult, and finally onto the spirituality category of an ebook store. It was not what she would have called a page-turner by any stretch of the imagination, but it was a handy repository of traditional witchery. Many of the chapters read like a spellbook, with compilations of different spells and charms, potions and talismans, for protection and good fortune and for banishing negative forces. Some were complex and intricate, requiring resources and rituals, while others were easy enough that she could have performed the spells there and then in the shop.

There was a spell – well, less of a spell, more of a practice – for honing one's ability to sense the spirit world. It was a straightforward practice, and simply required a quiet area for one to still the mind and feel the space around them. As the shop was still empty of any customers, Alice put down her phone, closed her eyes, and began to focus on taking slow, steady, deep breaths. After a few moments, she could feel herself easing into a tranquil, almost meditative, state of mind.

The door was suddenly thrust open, the bell clanging chaotically above it and rudely disrupting Alice's zen-like state. A frantic woman scurried in, a gold-looking vase held firmly under her arm. She hastened her way towards the counter, snaking through the winding aisles of antique furniture, and heading straight for Alice.

Alice stared, wide-eyed and worried, at the alarming woman approaching her. The old woman returned her gaze with a wild but haunted expression. 'I'd like to return this, please,' she spoke through laboured and panicked breaths, placing the vase on the counter-top along with the receipt.

'Certainly,' Alice said in the most calming voice

she could, giving the woman a cordial smile and glancing at the receipt. She picked up the vase, turning it over in her hands and tracing her fingers along the intricate patterns which decorated its body. There was a slight mark on the neck of the vase, which Alice rubbed at inquiringly, but the mark remained unchanged. Other than that, she couldn't see any breaks or imperfections; the vase was as close to being as good as new as it could possibly be. 'May I ask if there's a particular reason you're returning this, madam?'

'No, no,' the woman replied almost nervously, retrieving her purse from her handbag, 'I just want to get rid of it. Thank you.'

Politely nodding, Alice took the woman's receipt and her debit card, and began to run the transaction through the till. The cash drawer sprung open at a surprising speed, almost hitting her in the stomach and causing the coins to surge forwards in the tray like a wave. She slammed the drawer shut again, and swiped the card through the reader on the side of the till. The machine clunked and whirred as it printed off a scroll of a receipt.

'There we go, that's all done for you,' she paused, looking at the name on the debit card, 'Misses Roberts.' (She believed adding that personal touch made transactions feel less cold and mechanical). She slid the card and the receipt across the counter to her. 'Is there anything else I can help you with?'

'No,' Misses Roberts said, grabbing the receipt and her card, hastily stuffing them into the folds of her purse. She turned to leave and, seemingly having realised she'd forgotten her manners, quickly added, 'thank you,' before scurrying away.

'Have a good day,' Alice called after her, watching her with a mixture of curiosity and confusion. The little bell chimed as the woman walked out of the door. 'What a strange lady,' she mused, picking up the vase again. It gleamed beneath the light of the art deco lamp on the table, making the grooves and recesses of the carvings seem deeper and darker, the gold details shining even brighter. She tried to fix the cap back in place over the lip of the vase, but it refused to seal shut. 'I wish I knew what all that was about...'

With that, the bell above the doorway almost flew off of its fixture, clanging indelicately as the door was flung open once more. There stood Misses Roberts, a look of concern wrinkling her aged face. 'It's haunted,' she said, pointing an accusing finger to the ornament in Alice's hand.

'Excuse me?' Alice asked, bemused and blinking at the woman in the doorway.

'Bloody thing's cursed!' she continued, waggling her finger admonishingly at the vase. 'I want nothing to do with it, or its evil spirits.'

'Okay,' Alice said slowly, placing the vase carefully down upon the counter and warily stepping away from it. She knew better than to take any chances with allegedly cursed or haunted things. Smiling calmly at the woman, who remained anything but calm herself, Alice began to make her way around to the front of the counter. 'What makes you think the vase is cursed?'

'I'm sorry,' Misses Roberts said, addressing the floorboards as she looked down embarrassedly, shaking her head, 'I don't even know why I rushed back in here. I must seem like such a mad old bat to you. Don't listen to me. It's just been... Just been a really difficult week.' She turned and slowly started to make her way out of the door.

'Wait!' Alice called after her, darting forward and hurrying her way through the store's twisting aisles of antiques. 'Please wait, I really don't think you're mad.' Misses Roberts stopped in the middle of the doorway, turning to face the shop assistant dashing after her. 'I'm sorry it's been a difficult time for you, but I've had a fair few experiences with haunted things. Maybe I can help. Would you mind if I asked you a few questions about it?'

As much as she wanted to help this woman with whatever had clearly disturbed her, Alice would have been lying if she said she wasn't also a little bit excited to have discovered a new and curious case.

Misses Roberts hovered in the doorway for a moment. Not literally, of course, as a levitating lady would be an entirely separate supernatural situation. She simply stood on the threshold hesitantly, uncertain as to what to do with herself. For a second, Alice thought she was about to walk out of the door again, leaving her with a potentially cursed vase and no further information, which did not strike her as ideal. Thankfully, though, she eventually nodded her consent.

'You're a sweet girl,' she said, looking to Alice with a soft smile, 'of course you can. What's your name, love?'

'I'm Alice. What's yours?'

'Oh, I'm Deirdre,' said Deirdre.

'Well, it's a pleasure to meet you, Deirdre,' she replied with a smile, and gestured towards two large, comfortable-looking wing-back chairs in the corner of the store. 'Please, make yourself comfortable. Would you like a cup of tea?'

'Yes please,' Deirdre said as she eased herself into the comfort of the chair. The cushioned upholstery was as soft and welcoming as it looked. 'Just a splash of milk, please, thank you.' With a nod, Alice headed towards the back of the antique shop, and disappeared through the doorway behind the counter.

A few moments later, she returned bearing two mugs of tea, guiding a wooden stool with a few careful kicks to use as a small side-table. 'Here we go, cup of tea, just a splash of milk,' she reiterated as she placed the cups down on the stool, and sat herself in the other chair, sinking into its cushiony back.

'Thank you,' Deirdre said with a smile, reaching for her cup of tea and taking a sip, 'that's a lovely cuppa.'

When it came to haunted happenings, Alice had learned a thing or two; through first-hand experience, more often than not. She had watched Sam Hain work his peculiar methods of investigation on a number of occasions. Sometimes, he appeared to be the most knowledgable man in matters of magic and mystery; others, it seemed as if he was making everything up as he went along and was simply hoping for the best. In either case, Alice had seen the occult detective do his job enough times to have picked up some of his "technique." She too took a sip of her tea, and leaned slightly forwards in the chair.

'So, where shall we begin... When did you first notice something wasn't quite right about the vase?'

Deirdre took a sharp breath in between her teeth, pulling a face as if she had just sucked a lemon. 'It wasn't the vase itself, but everything that seemed to happen ever since I brought it into the house. About two weeks ago, I brought it home and gave it a good polish, and put it up on the mantelpiece in the living room. Looked really nice up there, too. I put some branches of magnolia blossom in it – you know, the pastel-pink and rich shades of magenta went well with the gilt patterns – it was really quite lovely.' She paused for a moment to drink her tea, although Alice could tell she was delaying having to repeat something unpleasant.

'Anyways,' she continued, 'my husband and I were having a bit of a difficult time. He stopped talking to me for a while, and I know Cedric can be a stubborn old fool at the best of times, but when I say he wasn't talking to me, I mean he did not make a peep. It was driving me loopy, and I told him so. Still he didn't say anything, so I told him I wished he'd just go boil his head. Then...'

She trailed off, and took another steadying sip of her tea. Her eyes appeared to well up. 'Not ten minutes later, he did make a noise. I heard him shrieking. So I rushed downstairs and into the kitchen and... And...'

Alice reached a reassuring hand forwards, lightly resting it on top of Deirdre's. 'It's okay,' she said in a comforting tone, although she was relatively certain what was coming next was anything but okay.

'I found him in the kitchen, leaning over the hob with his head in a pan of boiling water.' Deirdre's hands were shaking and her voice quavered. She closed her eyes as if trying to avoid seeing the image of that day again. 'You know,' she said, pointing to the tea, 'you've put just the right amount of milk in this. Is it semi-skimmed?'

'I'm so sorry,' Alice spoke softly. 'About your husband, I mean, not about the tea. But yes, it is semi-skimmed. Is he okay?' *What a bloody stupid question*, she immediately chastised herself, *of course he's not bloody okay. The man literally boiled his head.*

Deirdre nodded. 'Yeah, I dragged the silly bugger out and called an ambulance. Doctors say he's going to be fine eventually, just some scar tissue once his skin graft has healed. But he's doing well, thankfully. It's just... Just not something one expects to witness.'

'No, of course not,' Alice replied, her voice a low and sombre tone, 'but I'm glad to hear he's doing well, all things considered.' Even taking the allegedly cursed vase into account, she hadn't quite expected Deirdre's dialogue to take such a dark turn so soon. It had caught her off-guard, and she felt almost rude to talk more about the vase after this clearly traumatic event. 'So that was... We don't have to continue, if you don't want to? I mean, it's okay.'

'Oh bless your cottons,' Deirdre beamed, 'it's fine. You wanted to know about that blasted vase and its curse, and I want to tell you the story, so...'

'So you think the curse caused that?'

'Not immediately, no,' she continued, 'but a few days later I put two and two together, and made five, you see. I had been there with Ced in the hospital, but after a while I had to return home. I've still been visiting him, of course, but he didn't need me there day and night. Anyways, after a while in the house by myself, I was getting lonely. I was doing the cleaning, the cooking, sometimes talking to myself. And it was late one night – and I remember this, clear as day – I said to nothing in particular that I wished I wasn't so lonely, being there all by myself. Then this voice said, "you are not alone."' The old woman widened her eyes at Alice. 'Gave me the collywobbles.'

For a moment, Alice tried her hardest to suppress an amused smirk at the word "collywobbles." She had encountered more than a handful of haunting horrors, and "collywobbles" didn't even come close to conveying the sense of dread and foreboding such things can conjure. 'Are you sure the voice wasn't from someone outside, or next door, or on a TV or something?'

'Quite sure, dear. I heard it loud and clear as if

it was in the lounge. And it was. The voice was coming from that blasted vase.' She waggled her finger admonishingly in the vague direction of the offending object, and raised her voice as if she wanted it to know she was accusing it. Not that vases have ears with which to listen, but if it was indeed haunted or cursed, then calling it out might not be particularly wise. There was something about that vase which made Alice feel as if she was being watched, as if she and Deirdre were not the only ones in the shop. She shuddered.

Deirdre dropped to a conspiratorial tone, and leaned in towards Alice. 'It kept talking to me. Every night, I'd hear that damned voice whispering to me, keeping me awake. I saw things dancing in the shadows of the room, something almost like a heat-haze. I thought I was losing my mind, but it's all because of that vase, I'm sure of it.'

'I've experienced things similar,' Alice said, hoping she sounded calming. 'It can be downright terrifying, makes you feel like you're going mad, and it all feels so utterly unbelievable... But I believe you. And I believe that vase is somehow cursed.' Deirdre seemed to visibly relax, her face softening into a reassured smile. 'So after the voices started, you brought it back here?'

'I tried to bin it first. I put it out with my rubbish last Wednesday, but the binmen refused to take it. I had to ask my neighbour, Terrence – lovely boy, helped Ced and I replace our washing machine – if he would take it to the tip.'

'And I guess he refused to take it as well?'

'Oh no, Terrence is always asking if there's anything he can do for us. He's very sweet, and he was happy to help. He said he'd take it when he was next going to the tip. He's a landscape gardener, you see, so he's often dumping stuff for clients. Anyway, I think something must've happened between him and his partner. I haven't seen him about the past couple of days. Simon said that he just upped and left the other night and hasn't been in touch since.'

Resting her head against her hand and propping herself up with an elbow on the armrest, Alice could almost see the pieces slotting together in her mind. As she listened to Deirdre's testimony, she thought she was beginning to understand what was going on. The increasing tensions between Deirdre and Cedric, Terrence running out on Simon... It couldn't be a coincidence; *not that there is such a thing*, she thought. 'It almost sounds to me as if this curse is targeting relationships, with everything it started to put you and Cedric through when you first bought it. And now Simon and Terrence...'

Deirdre's eyes widened with shock. 'Do you think they're connected? That the curse affected them too?'

'Yes, I do,' she said. 'Wait, you didn't?'

'No, didn't cross my mind.'

For a moment, Alice didn't know how to reply. She would have thought that it stood to reason that if an object was cursed, exposing someone else to it would mean they suffer the curse too. *That's just plain and simple common sense, surely?*

Regardless, she felt as if she had an idea of what was going on. All that was needed now was a way to solve it.

'I'm not an expert on this sort of thing – curses, that is – I wouldn't know how to break it,' Alice said, looking over to the vase sitting by the till. After Deirdre's account, she could almost see an aura of something surrounding it, a faint haze drifting about the vase. Along with that uneasy sensation of being watched again. 'But I do know someone who might...'

CHAPTER II

'Well,' Sam Hain said, looking up from the vase, 'I have some good news, and I have some bad news.'

He had made his way to the antique shop the minute Alice had called. If there was a curse afoot, he hadn't a moment to lose. When he arrived, Alice briefed him with everything Deirdre had told her, and he immediately set about his craft.

Leaning across the counter, he had been trying to keep a safe distance from the vase as he examined it. If it was indeed cursed, the last thing he wanted to do was risk touching it. He'd used one of the magnifying glasses in the shop to more closely inspect the details and symbols across its surface, and although the geometry suggested that the patterns were intended for something more than simply looking pretty, he wasn't entirely sure what. The nine-pointed star on the cap seemed more indicative of a binding or summoning sigil than anything else. But other than that, and the lingering aura of magick, he couldn't divine precisely what its purpose was.

Sam had been working in almost complete silence for quite some time. The occasional "hmm" or "ah" had escaped his lips while he focused, but other than that he had offered very little insight into his thoughts. Now that he had announced he had news – good, bad, or otherwise – an even more tense silence hung in the air of the antique shop.

Deirdre looked at the occult detective expectantly. 'Well, aren't you going to tell us?'

'He enjoys the dramatic suspense,' Alice said. 'Give us the bad news first. Hopefully the good news will help soften it.'

'The bad news is: it doesn't appear to be as simple as a straightforward curse, but there is definitely some form of malign magick connected to this vase.' Sam waved the gleaming chrome body of the TechnoWand around the vase to demonstrate, carefully tracing its outline as if he was playing with a buzz-wire. The crystal at the wand's tip slowly began to glow, emitting a dim bluish light. Alice was used to seeing it shine decidedly brighter than this; there had been times it could've illuminated a whole room.

'Did you forget to put batteries in the thing?'

'No. This is fully charged. That's where the good news comes in. There's only a trace amount of magick in the aura surrounding the vase, almost like a metaphysical residue. It's as if its enchantment has been dissipated somehow, leaving behind only a footprint.'

'So it's not dangerous, then?' Alice asked. She hoped that this meant the problem was already resolved, before they even had to do anything about it. Maybe this incident had just been a weird blip, and – aside from the harm it had already caused the Roberts – it no longer presented a danger. She could hope, at least. Although something in the back of her mind told her things were never quite so nice and easy.

'I wouldn't risk touching it, just in case,' he replied, casting a wary eye in the vase's direction, 'but no. I don't think the vase poses any immediate danger.'

That's a relief, she thought. *Nothing to worry about, maybe the effects of the curse will just disappear on their own. There'd have been a "but" or a "however" if there was anything wrong.*

'The thing is-'

Fuck.

'-curses don't just tire themselves out and disappear. They need to be broken or rendered inert somehow,' Sam began to explain, leaning his elbow on an old pine chest of drawers. 'Now, maybe the full intention of the magick was achieved, so its purpose to exist ended with the satisfaction of a job well done. But if that was the case, I don't think we'd be able to detect any residue on the vase; the magick wouldn't linger, it would be spent. Gone. And from what you described, Deirdre, it manifested in a couple of different ways with you.'

'Yes, it did,' Deirdre chimed in. She seemed to be taking this all in her stride quite admirably, nodding along as Sam rattled on with his explanation, although her eyes frequently betrayed the haunted and perplexed thoughts running through her head. 'You know, everything with Ced and I, and then the voices...'

'Precisely,' he said with a snap of his fingers, 'connected, yet distinct, manifestations of magick. It's not behaving like a traditional, precise curse; more of a perversion of the Akashic field, manifesting misfortune. A dark and sinister twist of reality. It doesn't seem to be embodied by the vase like a traditional curse, either. Almost as if the vase was merely a receptacle for the magick. I think it's likely that this curse – or whatever it is – was *within* the vase, and released when the magickal seal was removed.'

'I'm sorry, dear,' Deirdre spoke, and she leaned forward in her chair, 'only half of that sounded like it made any sense.'

'I think,' Alice mused, standing up and pacing about the floor, 'it's a bit like spilling a bottle of water. The lid's come off, and – aside from a few drops left inside – the bottle is empty. But that doesn't mean the water's gone, it's just no longer in the bottle, meaning...'

'Meaning,' Sam finished the sentence, 'there's a big ol' soaking wet patch of spilt magick out there.'

The problem with magick being accidentally released – especially this kind of magick, with its malignant manifestations – wasn't just a matter of it being spilled. It was if it saturated an area; if that spillage would spread and leave a stain... It might be possible to mop up the worst of it, but if left too long that magick could seep in deeper. And, much like red wine soaking into a cream carpet, the damage and impact it caused could be irreparable.

Deirdre clutched at the sleeves of her blouse. All she had wanted to do was return the vase and be done with all this nonsense. She'd thought simply getting rid of the cursed ornament would be enough to make things okay again. Now she was faced with an antique seller and an urban wizard telling her she had unwittingly released a curse and spilled magick on north London. A nervous and uncertain fear coiled around her chest. 'I'm sorry,' she muttered, 'it's my fault for opening it. I didn't know.'

'Of course you didn't bloody know!' Sam said, almost humoured by the old woman's apology. 'I'd be infinitely more concerned if you'd opened it up with full knowledge of what would happen. That'd be a lot worse. Rest assured, this is no worse than an honest mistake with some unforeseen consequences.'

'It's okay,' Alice said, still adopting her most calming voice, 'we'll find a way to put things right.'

Sam was about to emphasise that they would do the best that they could. He didn't want to be giving Deirdre any false hope; short of breaking the laws of time, there was very little hope of them un-boiling Cedric's head, so that was already one thing that they wouldn't be able to put right. But before he even had the chance to say it, he was interrupted by the chiming of the bell above the door.

Fran Hendricks set foot in her shop, and looked around with a quizzical expression. It wasn't so much a matter of the people there, it was the manner in which they were positioned. An elderly woman (although she was probably younger than Fran herself) sat in a wing-back chair, and a young-ish man in a crumpled jacket and an old wide-brimmed hat was leaning nonchalantly on one of the chests of drawers. Meanwhile, her own employee, Alice, was leaning almost as casually, propped up against one of the dressers.

'If you're waiting for a bus,' she said, in way of announcing her arrival, 'you might be here a long time. They don't pass through the shop very often.'

Alice cleared her throat hastily. She pushed herself away from the dresser, moving in such a way that she hoped Fran wouldn't notice. 'Oh, hello, Fran. How was lunch? I was just-'

'Are you the proprietor?' Sam suddenly interrupted, adopting an exaggeratedly posh voice which sounded as if he'd failed an audition for *Downton Abbey*. He strode towards Fran, extending his hand to shake hers, although his fingers waved and flexed in an unusual fashion. 'Barnabus Hamptenfuppershire the Third. *Charmed.* I simply must commend you on some of your exquisite wares. It is a most *enchanting* shop.'

'Oh, well, thank you,' Fran said, not entirely sure what the appropriate etiquette was in the presence of a man of such prestige. She was honoured he had deemed to praise her quaint little establishment. 'I do the best with what I have. Is there anything that's caught your eye?'

'As a matter of fact, there is,' he said, pointing

to the vase upon the desk. 'I have that vase reserved for me to collect later. I ask that no-one touches it until I return, I want it in pristine condition.'

'Oh, right, that's marvellous,' Fran said, scampering around the counter, hurriedly scrawling a "Reserved: Do Not Touch" note and placing it down in front of the vase. 'It is a lovely piece, late nineteenth century,' she added, 'fine choice indeed.'

'Excuse me,' Deirdre spoke up, looking over to Alice, 'have we finished talking about the vase?'

Glancing over her shoulder, Alice watched as Fran busied herself around the man she believed to be Barnabus Hamptenfuppershire the Third. Bizarrely, she was fawning over every word her allegedly esteemed client was saying. 'I think so,' she mused, 'yes.'

'Oh, okay,' Deirdre said, easing herself up from the chair, 'it's just I'm meant to be meeting my friend, Amritam, for tea in a little bit. I hope you don't think I'm being rude.'

'No, of course not,' Alice replied with a reassuring smile, 'I don't think there's much more we can do here until Sam and I look into things a little more. After he's finished whatever this is...' She gestured vaguely in the direction of the occult detective, who was flamboyantly waffling on about early nineteenth century décor to an enraptured Fran Hendricks. 'If I can just take down your contact details, please, and your address. We'll see what we can do, and let you know what we find out.'

Deirdre nodded, retrieving a small organiser from her purse and a pair of reading glasses. 'Oh, thank you,' she said, placing the glasses on the bridge of her nose, and she began to recite her address and phone number. 'I won't be home until this evening,' she added, 'but you could see if Simon's experienced any of this you-know-what. Simon Melville. He's the house with the green door.'

'Thank you, we will do,' Alice said, dutifully tapping the last of the details into her phone. Once she was done, they said a quick goodbye, and Deirdre made her way out of the shop. 'Have a good afternoon,' she added, accidentally adopting her customer service voice, as Deirdre left.

'I was wondering if I might be able to borrow your most excellent assistant as well,' Sam's performance piece continued, gesturing towards Alice. She dreaded what improvised scenario he was about to rope her into. 'I would be interested in purchasing that cabinet also, however I am not sure whether it will fit in my home. Your assistant has talked me through your wares and my décor choices, and I would be honoured to have her opinion on some matters.'

'Do you feel you could help out this nice gentleman, Alice, love?'

'Of course,' she replied with a confused smile, 'I'd be happy to. I can work it into my break as well?'

'There's no rush,' Fran said, 'I can manage here.'

'Thank you,' Sam said, once again taking Fran's hand in a firm embrace, 'it is very much appreciated.' Still confused, Alice smiled her gratitude to Fran as well, and was swiftly led out of the store.

As soon as they were outside of the antique shop, and making their way down the alleyway towards the high street, Alice turned to Sam and asked, 'Right, just what the hell did you do there?'

'Oh, just a subtle charm spell,' he said casually, 'some ego-manipulation, a healthy dose of sounding authoritative, and – most importantly – making sure it's all over and done with so quickly she doesn't have a chance to notice I'm talking bollocks.' It was one of his oldest and most valuable skills, talking in such a way that nobody realised it was all bollocks. It had served him exceptionally well over the years. 'I've only been able to cast charms if they're for something quick and easy. Don't want to give the other person enough time to think about it too much.'

'Why? What happens if they think about it?'

'They often shout at me to leave their casino,' he said without missing a beat. He noticed the expression on Alice's face, and added, 'Don't worry, we were in and out of there as swiftly as possible. It'll probably barely even cross her mind now. Anyway, do you have the address?'

'Thank you, that's reassuring,' she said, although she hardly sounded convinced. 'And yes, I do.'

'Excellent. We'll hop on a bus up to Highbury.

If the curse is spreading, we should speak with the neighbours to be able to root it out. It sounds like the Melvilles were the last ones to come into contact with it, before Deirdre brought the vase back into the shop.'

'I was thinking about that,' Alice said, 'how it affected the Roberts first, then the Melvilles. Whatever it is, that vase caused tensions between Deirdre and Cedric, and then the neighbour's husband just left one night... It seems like its a curse which targets relationships.' She paused. They crossed the road to the other side of the high street, and made their way towards the bus stops. 'I'm not sure where the talking shadows fit in with that, but the fact this alleged curse affected both the Roberts' and the Melvilles' marriages can't be a coincidence, surely?'

'No such thing,' he said with a wry smile, 'they're bound to be connected. I'm not an expert on this sort of thing – relationships, that is – but it sounds like a solid theory.' He looked up at the digital board of bus arrivals. The next one towards Highbury was only a minute away. 'We'll soon find out more, and hopefully nip this thing in the bud before it has a chance to take hold.'

Terrence and Simon Melville lived next door to the Roberts' household, along a quiet and quite unassuming residential street somewhere in the middle of Highbury. It was the very image of an idyllic suburban road, with its tall and narrow Edwardian terraced houses, well-kept front gardens, and perfectly adequate roadside parking.

On the surface of things, the fact that a malignant curse had taken hold here would be quite unbelievable. *For the time being*, Sam thought. *The original irruption may go unnoticed, but if left unresolved, it can plant its roots deep and spread.*

'This is the place,' Alice said, looking up from the map on her phone to the red-brick property with the green front door before them. The garden wall was lined with a modest hedgerow, and a collection of flowers ran alongside the path towards the front door. A welcoming pot of petunias sat on a shelf above the neatly stacked recycling bins just inside of the porch. Through the frosted glass panels of the door, they could glimpse the distant orange glow of light coming from further within. 'Looks like someone's home, too.'

They strode up the garden path towards the door, politely wiping their feet on the doormat as Sam knocked a firm and rhythmic knock. For a moment there was only silence, but then the distant sound of feet walking down stairs reached their ears. Through the frosted glass, they could see the indistinct shape of a person descending and making their way towards the door.

'Hello?' asked a man in his late-forties, wearing a particularly crumpled-looking shirt, peering his head out of the open door. 'Can I help you?'

'As a matter of fact, no,' Sam replied, 'but we were hoping we might be able to help you.'

The man in the doorway seemed relieved. His face visibly relaxed, and he opened the door wider for his two visitors. 'Are you here about Terrence?'

'Actually, yes, we are. We heard about-'

'Oh thank goodness,' the words fell from his mouth in a sigh of relief. 'I'm Simon. Simon Melville. I was hoping someone would show up. Please, do come in.' Simon stepped back and ushered Sam and Alice inside, gently closing the door behind them.

Inside, the house was as idyllic and homely as it had appeared on the outside. Just inside of the doorway, an array of coats – both adult and child-sized – and tote bags hung from the wall. Beneath them was a short wooden bench which housed everyone's shoes and trainers, although a couple of them had escaped and lay about the floor. On the opposite wall was a wide mirror, which reflected light coming in through the door along the length of the hall. A long woven rug stretched along the polished wooden floor of the hallway, just to the side of the staircase, welcoming them inwards. The smell of fresh baking wafted through the air and greeted their nostrils.

As they stepped over the threshold, Sam and Alice again wiped their feet on the "Home Is Where The Heart Is" doormat, took off their shoes and politely placed them on the shoe bench.

'I didn't want to report my husband was missing too soon. No point causing a kerfuffle if it's all much ado about nothing. But I know Terrence, and I know he wouldn't just walk out like this,' Simon said as he guided Sam and Alice towards the kitchen at the back of the house. The two of them exchanged perplexed glances at one another. 'I'm glad the police responded so quickly.

Although, I must admit, I wasn't expecting you to look so informal when I opened the door; I'd have thought you'd be in uniform.'

'Aha, yes,' Sam said through a grimace, looking to Alice, 'we're, um... We're not actually uniformed patrol officers.' If Simon had been looking, he would almost certainly have seen the cogs whirring in Sam's head as he desperately tried to cover for himself and Alice. 'We're plain clothes detectives. Helps us look into missing persons far more discreetly.'

Simon turned to Sam and Alice. He looked them both up and down, narrowing his eyes into what appeared to be a sceptical squint, as if he was scanning for the authenticity of their statement. 'All right,' he said, and ushered them through the door into the kitchen.

The polished wooden floor followed through from the hallway into the open space of the kitchen-diner. A modern cooking area occupied one side of the room, all brushed steel appliances and gleaming white counter tops. By the side of the sink, a pile of dirty dishes sat waiting to be loaded into the dishwasher. A collection of crayon drawings were prominently displayed on the fridge, presumably the artwork of either a child or an abstract-expressionist on a budget.

Dividing this from the dining area was a long kitchen island, a recently used coffee percolator in the middle. On the other side of the room was an oaken dining table, coated in a dark green tablecloth, and large enough to sit around eight or ten people.

'Please, make yourselves comfortable,' Simon said, indicating for Sam and Alice to take a seat. 'Would either of you care for a cup of tea, or coffee?'

'A tea would be lovely, if you're making one,' Sam said, pulling back one of the dining chairs from around the long table and taking a seat. A warm and gentle breeze came drifting in through the open back door, carrying with it the soft clucking sound of chickens. Gazing idly out at the back garden, at its bright flowerbeds and verdant green hedges, Sam watched as a small flock of chickens contently milled about the lawn, hopping around their coop.

'Tea for me too, please,' Alice said, sitting down next to Sam.

Within moments, Simon came and joined them both at the table, carrying a rustic blue teapot and three matching cups. He placed the cups down in front of each of them and poured the tea, before dashing back to the kitchen. Picking up a small milk jug and a plate of home-made cookies, he carried them over and sat down opposite Sam and Alice. 'I baked these this morning,' he said, sliding the plate to the middle of the table, 'I've been doing a lot of stress-baking these past couple of days. Gives me something to focus on. And I thought the children deserved something nice to come home to after school.'

'How are the children handling what's happened?' Alice asked.

'They're not,' was Simon's simple answer. 'I'm worried about them. As if there wasn't already enough to worry about.' He took a sip of tea. 'I don't know if they're in denial, or they just don't know how to process it... They just keep saying things like "no, he's not, Daddy's in the garden." No matter how much I try to talk with them about it, they refuse to acknowledge it. Anyway...' He gestured to the plate of cookies. 'Please, help yourselves.'

Sam didn't need to be told twice. He happily helped himself to one of the cookies with a polite "thank you," and took a bite. It was soft, warm, and just the right balance of dense and doughy as his teeth sunk into it. 'Delicious,' he mumbled through a mouthful of salted caramel. Dusting the crumbs from his fingers and taking a sip of his tea, Sam cleared his throat. 'So, in regards to your husband, could you talk us through the events which led to Terrence's disappearance.'

For a moment, it seemed as if Simon had become frozen in time. He sat there, motionless and silent, his eyes glazing over as he stared vacantly into a space beyond the cup of tea before him. A noise grated in his throat.

'I don't know where to begin. It all seemed perfectly normal. It was Saturday, and I'd finished going over some documents a lot sooner than I'd expected to. Terry had the weekend off, too, and the weather was nice, so we took the kids out for a picnic and a kick around at Highbury Fields. We came home, Terry made tapas – it was his turn to cook; mine to clean – and we relaxed in front of the television until it was time to put Toby and Katie to bed. While I was doing the dishes, Terry

went to tell the kids a bedtime story, and then...'
He trailed off, gazing back into the abyss of his
teacup. 'I didn't see him after that.' Habitually, he
fiddled with his phone on the tabletop, glancing at
the lockscreen as if he were expecting a
notification. There was none.

'I'm so sorry,' Alice said, reaching her hand out
across the table to him, 'I can't imagine what you
must be going through.'

Simon smiled weakly towards her. 'Thank you.
It's horrible, not knowing what happened to him. I
just wish something could give me an answer.' He
picked up one of the cookies and slowly took a
bite. Alice had never really ascribed emotions to
the way people eat, but – looking at Simon – she
could see that this was a man who was chewing
forlornly.

From somewhere around their feet, there came
a soft and arrhythmic tapping noise. It sounded
scattered, almost a staccato of clicks against the
wooden floor – slow and then suddenly in short,
fast bursts – mixed with the occasional clucking.
Something pecked at the hem of Simon's trouser
leg. Placing the cookie next to his teacup, he
leaned down, disappearing below the table. 'Come
here, baby,' he said in a kindly whisper, emerging
from beneath the tabletop with a chicken held
between his hands.

'Who's this then?' Sam spoke in a cartoonishly
high pitched voice. He reached his hand out to the
chicken, who promptly nipped inquisitively at his
fingers.

Settling the bird down in his lap and softly

stroking its feathers, Simon said, 'Oh, to be honest with you, I wouldn't know one from the other. They were always more Terry's babies. But this one's become a cuddler these past few days. Haven't you, sweetheart?' His voice changed timbre as he directed his attention to the chicken. 'Must know something's wrong.'

'That's so sweet,' Alice said, smiling at the ginger-feathered bird peeking its head just above the edge of the table. 'I've often found animals can be so in-tune with their owner's feelings. They always seem to know when something's not right.'

'Definitely, I know what you mean. And you certainly do, don't you?' Simon said, again changing his cadence as he looked lovingly at the chicken in his lap, who gave a contented cluck in response. A glimmer of an amused smile crossed his lips, a subtle chuckle jumped in his throat. 'Although I wouldn't say we're their owners... These lot certainly know who rules the roost around here, and it's not me or Terry.'

'Glad to hear you've got a strict pecking order here,' Sam interjected with a grin so broad there was no hiding how terribly proud he was of that pun. The other two smiled in polite amusement at him, although it sounded as if the chicken chuckled. Beneath the table, Sam gently nudged Alice's leg with his knee.

'Yeah, I got it,' she said, again flashing a polite smile at him, although her eyes couldn't quite hide her mild irritation at his apparent need for attention.

With a cautionary glance across the table, Sam

made sure that their host wasn't looking. Thankfully, a lot of Simon's attention was directed towards his feathered friend. Confident that he wasn't being watched, Sam attempted to communicate through a complex series of facial expressions. 'No, I know,' he said, widening his eyes and repeatedly shifting them down and to the side, while his eyebrows waggled like hyperactive caterpillars on his forehead. 'It was just low-hanging fruit, I wanted to make sure it hadn't passed beneath.' His mouth tugged sideways as he tilted his head down, as if a fishing hook had caught in his cheek and someone was trying to reel him in.

Following the absurd directions Sam had been trying to give her, Alice glanced down just under the table. While she and Simon had been discussing the emotional capacity of chickens, Sam had discreetly pulled the transphasic probe from his pocket and had been scanning the Akashic field. Evidently the probe had detected something, as when Alice looked down she could see the glow from the TechnoWand illuminating the space beneath the table. Somehow, the light emitting from the wand's crystalline tip was simultaneously emitting shades of icy blue and white.

'What does it mean?' she mouthed silently to him.

'No idea,' he mouthed back.

A cold chill ran down her spine, tingling across her skin. She shook the feeling off.

'Anyway, enough about chickens,' Simon said,

turning his attention back to the two of them, unaware of the glowing magical device beneath his dining table. As discreetly as he had first withdrawn it, Sam carefully secreted the probe up his sleeve. 'How can I help with your investigation?'

'Well, firstly, we're going to need to build a bit of a profile around Terrence,' Sam began, resting his elbows on the table and clasping his hands together intently. The TechnoWand slid comfortably further up his sleeve, safely out of sight. 'We'll probably need to take a bit of a look around, and ask you a few more questions, if that's okay.'

Although almost all semblance of emotion had drained from Simon's face as he listened, he nodded his consent. 'Very well,' he said, his voice plain and stoic, although it sounded like it had caught in his throat.

'Excellent,' Sam declared, clapping his hands together and pushing his chair back. Its legs groaned as they scraped across the floor. As he stood up, the occult detective adjusted his jacket, performatively fiddling with the lapels as he attempted to discreetly slide the wand into his breast pocket again. He angled his arm just so inside his jacket, and the device slid down his sleeve. It dropped, gliding past his fingers as it landed securely in his pocket.

Nailed it.

Meanwhile, somewhere in Highbury...

'Hey, hey, come back here, young lady!' Daniel called after his daughter as she stomped up the stairs. Jess had seemed surly and distant the moment she had walked through the door. It had been a bit of an ongoing theme the past few days, but her irritability and evasiveness were starting to wear thin for him. 'We need to talk things out.'

'What's the point?' she shouted back at him. Jess was in her mid-teens, and she made a point of reminding her father of that at every given opportunity. 'You're only going to send me to my room anyway. Might as well cut the bullshit and go there myself.'

She had recently discovered punk and, along with the music and fashion, a new sense of freedom and individuality. As well as a healthy disrespect for authority. As far as she was concerned, she was living her own life, making her own choices, and didn't need her father coddling her any more. She wasn't wrong, of course, she was living her life and growing into herself beyond being Daniel's daughter. However, the teething phase of her newfound liberty had caused the two of them to butt heads quite frequently. Regardless of her rebellious streak, he considered himself lucky that Jess was the teenager he'd had – Daniel remembered all too well what he had been like at her age – but even so, there were times when she seemed to be fifteen-going-on-five.

Daniel sighed, a long and tired sigh. For a moment, he thought wistfully back to the days when she really was five. When the most important things in her life were Lego, cartoons and a good bedtime story, usually involving witches. Now her priorities were all boys, parties, listening to music at volumes which had caused the neighbours to complain on more than one occasion, and doing her best to avoid her dad. Things had been much easier before.

'I wish you'd just talk to me,' he said to the air at the top of the stairs, just as Jess's door slammed loudly behind her. It seemed futile speaking to the empty space, especially as it was likely only a few moments away from being filled with the sound of the Sex Pistols, but he had to at least try. 'I want to know what's going on with you lately.'

The door creaked open again, and footsteps scuffed their way back towards the top of the stairs. She stood there, looking down at her father, her arms folded and lips pouted. 'What?' she said, more aggressively than she had intended. 'What do you mean, "what's going on lately"?'

'I just...' He hadn't quite expected her to come back. Pausing to think for a second, Daniel tried to choose his next words carefully, lest they end up in an argument. Again. 'You've just seemed a little distant lately,' he said, before hastily adding, 'and I know you want your own space sometimes, and I get that, that's cool. But it seems like something's troubling you, and you're trying to avoid me. Is it something I've done? Is anything bothering you?'

'What's bothering me is you giving me the third degree!' Jess stamped her feet uncomfortably at the top of the stairs. Despite herself, her stand-offish demeanour began to waiver, her expression softening. 'It's not you,' she said quietly, 'nothing you've done. It's just... You wouldn't understand.'

'Try me,' her father said with a kindly smile, sitting on the step halfway up the stairs and patting the spot next to him. Much to his surprise, she took a few steps down and sat next to him.

'Okay, well, it's this boy-'

'Uh-huh,' Daniel nodded knowingly.

'If you could roll your eyes any harder you'd be looking at your own brain.'

'Sorry, please continue.'

Jess made a sound that was partway between a grunt and a sigh. 'So, his name's Scott. I like him, right? And apparently he likes me. But I text him over the weekend, and he hasn't messaged me back. He's been online, but he still hasn't messaged me.'

'These things happen, he might just be busy,' Daniel said, and almost immediately regretted the words as they fell out of his mouth. 'I had a similar thing when I was your age, and these things work themselves out eventually. Not that we had text messages or the internet then, so it wasn't all so immediate, but-'

'It's not similar at all!' Jess interrupted, her voice rising as she stood up again. 'I knew you wouldn't understand. I wish you knew what it felt like!'

Daniel spluttered. It caught him entirely off-guard, almost choking as a feeling welled up in his chest, like a heavy stone weighing on his heart. His eyes began to water, and beyond his control he let out a pained whimper. Jess's dramatic exit was put on hold. She turned around and sat back down.

'Dad, are you... Are you crying?'

'No,' he croaked.

'Yes, you are,' she said, 'what the hell's wrong with you?'

For reasons beyond his understanding, Daniel began to sob. He rested his head in his hands as he felt his face flush red, the hot sting of tears rolling down his cheeks and a particularly gooey sensation clogging his nose. 'I just don't understand why Scott can't text you back?' he cried. 'You deserve someone who would always make time for you.' He threw his arms around Jess in a tight hug. She uncertainly patted his shoulder. 'And you two would be so cute together!' he wailed.

'I know, right?!' Jess began to cry too, although she felt a strange relief washing over her. It was as if a heaviness had been lifted from her as the flood gates opened, and she allowed her emotions to come spilling out. Pent up sadness, anxiety, and a bit of jealous resentment, bubbled their way up to the surface and were released. Tears ran down her face as she heaved a sob.

Father and daughter held each other in their arms, leaning on one another for support as they cried together. Both feeling more than a little confused as to why any of this was happening.

CHAPTER III

Simon had led Sam and Alice upstairs to the first floor. If the entryway and kitchen-dining area which had first greeted them had seemed homely, the upstairs living space only added to the feeling. In their time living in Highbury, the Melvilles had certainly managed to make a house a home. It would be easy to imagine it being featured in an ideal home magazine, if a bit more lived-in than most model homes.

On the landing, framed holiday photographs of the family – Simon, Terry, and their two children at several different destinations, from Disneyland to Venice – decorated the walls. Colourful woven rugs stretched across the wooden floor, leading to the rustic bare-wood doorways of each of the rooms.

'Through there's my home office,' Simon said, waving his hand towards the open doorway at the far end, through which they could see a large desk covered with files and paperwork. 'Terry always says I work too much, bringing it home and never really having any time off, but you know what they say... Justice never sleeps.'

'Would you say you're a bit of a workaholic

then?' Alice asked, trying to gauge just how much work was in fact piled on the desk. From where she was standing, it seemed to be quite substantial.

'Me? No, no,' Simon shook his head, 'I wouldn't say so. You ask my husband, on the other hand, he'd say I never relax.'

'Was that a point of contention between the two of you?' Sam enquired. If Alice's hunch that the curse was causing rifts in relationships, he wanted to identify any potential weak spots the magick might manipulate. 'If it feels like you're always working, I can imagine that must put a strain on your home life.'

With his hand resting on the door handle to the bedroom, Simon stood motionless for a moment. His head hung down as he exhaled. 'We might have argued about it, every now and again,' he said, the sound of remorse heavy in his voice. 'I know I can get caught up in my work, and sometimes it takes away time from being with the family. On more than one occasion, Terry's told me he missed me, even if I've been home all weekend, because I've seemed distant or wrapped up in the work.' He sighed. 'But what can you do? Being a lawyer isn't something I can just turn off after a nine-to-five at the office.'

He began to turn the handle, and slowly pushed the door open. 'That's the irony, of course,' he added, 'all that time I wasn't with my family due to working so much. Now the thought of even opening a file while my husband is missing makes me sick to the pit of my stomach. And I need to be one hundred percent present and here for Toby and Katie through this, too.' Holding the door open for the two of them, he gestured for them to enter. 'Anyway, the master bedroom. I apologise for the mess.'

Sam and Alice stepped across the threshold into the master bedroom. If the rest of the house looked like an ideal home, it was because the chaos had been confined to the bedroom. It would have been a spacious and minimalist arrangement, were it not for the clothes strewn about the floor. The laundry basket lay on its side in the corner. The bed remained unmade, the sheets in an untidy bundle at the foot of the bed, the pillows unplumped and in a pile to one side. Empty cups which had once been filled with tea sat on one of the bedside cabinets, a book and a mobile phone rested on top of the other.

'I... Haven't exactly been keeping on top of things. The housework has somewhat fallen by the wayside these past few days.'

'That's understandable,' Alice said, 'you've got more on your mind than worrying whether the bed is made or not.' She glanced about the room, the disarray looking like more than just a couple of days worth of neglect, but she wasn't one to judge; her bedroom was often in a state even on a good day.

Sam didn't pay much attention to the state of the room. His focus had been drawn to something else. Something which might suggest events more untoward, maybe even more unnatural, than a husband simply walking out. He stared fixedly at the phone on the bedside cabinet. Earlier on, downstairs in the kitchen, he had noticed Simon idly checking a phone, and he very much doubted he was a man who had need for more than the one.

'Terry's phone, I presume?' he asked, indicating the device on the cabinet, and Simon nodded. 'Generally speaking, if someone was planning on going somewhere for any reason, I'd assume they'd at least take their phone with them.'

'That's what I thought, too,' he agreed. 'Terry wouldn't just leave without taking his mobile. He'd need to use it for maps, and to call people, and for emergencies, and...' He cut himself off mid-sentence, pinching the bridge of his nose. 'It's just yet another thing which doesn't make sense in this nightmare.'

'So he didn't express any intent to go anywhere at all lately? Nothing that might've suggested he would just take off like this?'

'If he did, don't you think I would have tried to go looking for him?' Simon raised his voice, affronted that such a question was even being asked of him. He caught himself, took a breath, and apologised. 'I'm sorry, it's not your fault. I know you've got to cover all the grounds to help, but it's frustrating, and heartbreaking. I don't know what to do.'

Taking a few more steadying and calming breaths, Simon continued, 'No, he didn't say anything about going anywhere. Nothing which seemed out of the ordinary, anyway. The only places he'd mentioned going were us on holiday to Aruba, or taking some of the garden waste to the tip later this week. Apparently next door wanted a couple of things dumped when he was next heading up that way.'

Deirdre's cursed vase, Alice thought, *if only they knew how much trouble that ornament was going to cause them.*

Pacing around the end of the bed, carefully stepping around and over the clothes, and approaching the bedside cabinet, Sam asked, 'And I guess it would be daft to ask if you've checked his phone for anything unusual?' He picked up the phone, glancing at the lockscreen. Behind the pattern lock was another picture of the family, all together and huddled up to fit in the frame. *Terry was clearly a very family-oriented man*, he thought, *it's unlikely he'd leave his phone behind, and even more unlikely he'd leave his family.*

'I did, yes. I didn't see anything strange or out of the ordinary, though,' he answered. It appeared that for a moment Simon was weighing something up in his mind, debating whether to say something or not, before he suddenly blurted, 'It's a capital-T, by the way. From the bottom, to the right and then left. In case you wanted to check yourself.'

Sam obliged, swiping his thumb up, to the right and to the left. The screen unlocked. He wasn't sure what he expected to find, or indeed what he should be keeping an eye out for, but he scrolled through some of the data on Terry's phone. As far as he could tell, there was nothing in particular which stood out to him as being noteworthy. Messages all seemed fairly run-of-the-mill, emails were the usual mix of notifications, newsletters and spam, and the recent search history primarily seemed to be about tracking down what other films particular actors had been in.

There was only one more thing he wanted to try. Not wanting to be too obvious, he tried to signal Alice by waggling his fingers about; it didn't represent anything, but he hoped it was odd enough to cue her.

Alice noticed Sam waving his fingers, as if he was either a magician at a children's party or a puppeteer without a puppet. It wasn't abundantly clear what he was trying to say, but she inferred he probably wanted Simon's attention drawn elsewhere for a moment. 'I don't want to seem like I'm prying,' Alice said. Simon turned to face her, and she looked at him with an empathetic smile. 'You don't have to answer anything you don't feel comfortable with, but it might help. You mentioned earlier how your workload was a point of contention sometimes. Did you argue with each other at all in the past week? Any disagreements?'

'No, we didn't. I can hardly say Terrence and I are perfect; of course we have our moments, but we always make up afterwards. Always,' he replied. 'So even if we did argue, Terry wouldn't just walk out. But we hadn't, and it just makes it all the more confusing and concerning.'

Meanwhile, with Simon's back turned, Sam had fished the TechnoWand from out of his jacket and was waving it around the phone. He tried simply moving it up and down, but nothing. He tried circling the device, and nothing. He even tried winding a spiral around the device, as if he was spooling a length of invisible string, and still there was nothing. Not even the faint glimmer or flicker of a trace amount of Akashic energy. He shrugged in Alice's direction.

'And you said Terry went to tell the children a story. Would you mind if we had a quick look in the children's rooms?' Alice asked.

'It's just the one room, actually,' Simon said, 'but of course. It's just up the stairs here.' He walked them both out of the bedroom, and up the stairs to the top floor of the house.

'Other than the fact your husband suddenly vanished,' Sam pressed as they ascended the staircase, 'was there anything else unusual that you noticed that night? Anything either related to Terry, or anything strange but seemingly unconnected? Anything and everything could be important.'

'The only thing that stands out strangest in my mind is the fact that he didn't take anything with him, or even leave a note. His keys, wallet, phone, favourite jacket, shoes... All of it, still here. Anyway,' he ushered the two of them towards the doorway. The names "Katie" and "Toby" were spelled out on little wooden signs which hung from the door.

It might have been the first time either Sam or Alice had seen a child's bedroom tidier than that of their parents. Especially considering the space was shared by two children. Which isn't to say it was pristinely clean and tidy, but it was at least in a better state than Simon had left the master bedroom. Clothes were clustered around a basket, although not quite making it as far as inside, instead draped over the rim. A handful of toys lay discarded across the floor, and a collection of drawings were piled next to a table, but beyond that everything else seemed relatively ordered. Even the beds had been made, although it did appear the children had done so themselves in a rush.

While Simon stood in the doorway, Sam and Alice paced about the room. They cast their eyes over action figures and dolls, over the half-complete Lego model on an adorably tiny table top, and at the collection of drawings piled on the floor next to it. Nothing immediately caught their attention, though.

'You know,' Simon mused, 'there was another thing. When I talked to Toby and Katie that night, after... Well, after Terry didn't come back, they said he was afraid.'

'Afraid? In what way?' Alice asked.

'I honestly don't know. He wouldn't have been telling them a scary story, not at that time of night, so I know he wouldn't have been putting on an act for them.'

She knelt down on the floor, and began to look at the drawings. Children, she figured – recalling the dissertation she wrote while at university on the topic of art as a medium of expression and psychological interpretation – might draw something representing whatever happened that night. Something as prominent as their father disappearing was bound to have made an impact. As she rummaged through the drawings, she found depictions of a house, figures presumably representing their family (happy, together, and beneath a big smiling sun), and some scrawled illustrations of chickens. Nothing, she concluded, which yielded any insight into the complex emotional state of a child.

'Well, did either of them elaborate? Anything that might at least hint to what he said or did?' Sam asked.

'Katie's been very distant, and spent most of yesterday out in the garden. Toby just seems to think it's one big joke.' He sighed a sigh which almost sounded as frustrated as it did forlorn. 'Terry would've told me if something was bothering him, surely? We've always known we can turn to each other and work through things together, no matter what. I don't think that would change now.'

Ponderously stroking his chin, Sam mused. Nothing seemed to be quite adding up in his mind. The fact the man had vanished without a trace, without a word, leaving behind his belongings, suggested he wasn't acting of his own free will. Based on the way Simon talked about Terry, too, he wouldn't just walk out, which – to him, at least – implied magick was at play. But it wasn't quite the same magick, the suspected relationship curse, which had fraught Deirdre and Cedric; otherwise, Terry and Simon would've at least argued before the former's sudden disappearance. Very little about their case bore any similarity to the story Deirdre had first told Alice. And now, with the tenuous thread of Terry's terror, things were only growing murkier. Either something coerced Terry to leave, or something took him by force...

'Do you,' Sam began, the words still formulating in his mind as he spoke, 'believe it might be possible that someone – or something – may have taken Terry against his will?'

Simon's eyes started to well up. 'It had crossed my mind,' he croaked, 'but I just... It just seems impossible, right?'

'Improbable, perhaps, but not entirely impossible,' Sam stated. As far as statements go, this was not a particularly reassuring one for Simon.

'But how?' Simon seemed almost confrontational. 'It's the top floor of the house! And why?'

'Those are two very good questions,' Sam said, adopting what he hoped was a knowledgeable tone, 'and two questions I hope we can answer for you.'

While the two of them were talking, something had caught Alice's eye. She had turned to stand up when she noticed it, just beneath one of the beds and in the shadows. Scuffling herself along the carpet on her knees, she peered under the bed.

It was like another world under there. Tucked away deep in the shadow of the bed, small clumps of dust clung to the carpet, seemingly unreachable by any hoover. Several die-cast toy cars lay scattered about, some upturned, and a couple of action figures lay by the side of them. The scale may not have been precisely in proportion, but glancing at this vignette almost resembled a post-apocalyptic landscape; a landscape made all the more surreal by the presence of a number of old, forgotten socks. *A-sock-alypse,* Alice amused herself, before reaching into the space beneath the bed.

When her hand returned from the shadows, she held something small and orange between her thumb and forefinger. She held it up in the light to get a better look at the thing. A small, fluffy, chicken feather.

'Ah,' Simon said, happy for the sudden distraction from the topic at hand, 'the chickens sometimes roam the house as they please.' He smiled. 'As you probably already noticed, they're really a part of the family. Terry insisted they be treated as if they were our more feathery children.'

With that, the sound of a phone ringing came trilling from downstairs. Turning and starting to hurry down to answer it, Simon called back, 'Sorry, I'll be back in a moment.'

Alice let the feather glide gently back to the ground as she stood up, dusting off her hands. 'So,' she said, craning her neck to see if Simon had moved out of earshot. He was nowhere to be seen. 'What are your thoughts and theories so far? Because honestly, I'm feeling a little stumped.'

Sam sucked air through his teeth. 'Frustratingly, likewise.'

'This is normally the moment you have some grand epiphany and ramble to yourself while people politely pretend to listen!' she exclaimed. 'You can't have nothing, surely?'

'Oh no, I don't have nothing,' he said, standing straight and adjusting his lapels with an air of self-importance. 'In fact, I have a great many things. The problem is, there seems to be one big glaring hole in the middle of it all preventing them from coming together. And then there's this.' He held the TechnoWand up for her to see. The crystal at its tip glowed with the same bright, bluish-white aura as it had done downstairs in the kitchen.

'Well, that's something, at least,' she said, 'what does it mean?'

'No idea,' Sam droned, still waving the transphasic probe about. 'The bit that baffles me is, if this is a result of Deirdre accidentally releasing a curse, and its effects were spilling over, then the Akashic disturbance should be fairly consistent. But it's not. It seems localised, specifically here and in the kitchen, but not anywhere in between.'

'See, now you're starting to ramble while you think out loud,' Alice joked, playfully nudging his arm. 'You might talk yourself towards an epiphany in a minute.'

'Well, there's one thing we can know for sure, and that there's definitely some kind of magick at work here. The probe, Terry's sudden and unprovoked disappearance, not to mention how all of his belongings are still here. Nor how he's not the kind of man who would just up and leave his family... It all points to some external force. Whether something took him, or it made him do something he normally never would do, I don't know. And how does it connect to Deirdre and Cedric?'

'Well, Cedric boiling his own head doesn't exactly seem like something someone would normally do, does it? Sounds quite out of character for most people, if you ask me. Seems like something was compelling them both to act against their better judgement.'

Sam clicked his fingers. 'That's an excellent point. Yes.' He continued clicking his fingers, rapidly and repeatedly, as he thought. He would say it helped him think; many would say it was profoundly annoying. 'So we're dealing with something which compelled these two men to act out of character. Something Cedric wasn't aware of, but somehow Terry was? If the children are right about him being afraid of something. But what? And why? And there's our hole again. We figure out the missing piece, and the rest should all fall into place. Maybe Deirdre's house has more answers.'

'Wait a minute,' Alice said, pointing towards the TechnoWand, which continued to prominently glow, 'doesn't that thing normally make a noise? Like a humming sound?'

Looking at the probe in his hand, Sam nodded. 'I imagine it would be humming right now, yes,' he agreed, 'but I put it on silent. I didn't want Simon to know whenever I've been trying to read the Akashic field; there'd be too many difficult questions.'

'Of course your wand can be put on silent...

Let me guess, it has an aeroplane mode too?'

'Kind of. You have no idea how many times I've been stopped by airport security...'

'Oh, no,' Alice said with a knowing tone, slowly nodding her head. 'I can imagine.'

The sound of footsteps coming back up the stairs reached their ears, and Sam hastily shoved the probe back into his pocket. Simon had already been through enough as it was, without having an occult detective explain the preternatural potentials to this case. He doubted learning that magickal forces were at work would provide the man with much comfort or reassurance. They both turned to face the door as the footsteps drew closer.

'Sorry about that,' Simon said as he rounded the top of the stairs, 'that was my mother calling to see... Well, you know.' He offered them a weak smile. 'It's sweet she keeps checking in, but every time I have to tell her nothing's changed it hurts my heart. I can keep it together, mostly, but whenever I have to talk about it...'

'Yeah, I can imagine,' Alice said softly, reaching out and giving Simon's arm a reassuring rub. 'We really appreciate you taking the time to talk to us about this, and walk us through things.'

'Of course,' he muttered, 'anything... Anything that helps you get to the bottom of this, and bring my love home safely.'

'I assure you, we will do everything in our power to come to a conclusion,' Sam said.

'Thank you,' Simon bowed his head. Even

though neither Sam or Alice had offered him any insights or answers, he still felt reassured by their promise to help. 'I don't know what else I can provide you with, but if there's anything else that might help the investigation...'

'We've got a good idea of Terry's character, and a timeline of your side of events around that night, so that's a start,' Sam said, 'now we just need to start working with the details you've given us.'

'The minute we find out something about Terry's situation, you'll be the first to know,' Alice offered Simon a comforting smile, and he nodded his appreciation.

'We might need to talk to your neighbours, too, just in case anything else may have been seen or heard that night,' Sam added. *And hopefully there'll be more answers in the place where this magick was first unleashed.*

CHAPTER IV

Sam and Alice stood outside of the Roberts' residence, staring at the building as if it was a roadblock. Deirdre still wasn't home, and neither of them could blame her; when there was the risk of one's own house being cursed with malign magick, it's generally wise to avoid it. After impersonating a police office (albeit only through omission), and to a lawyer no less, Sam was not inclined to add breaking and entering to his list of crimes for the day.

The problem was, of course, that this meant that their investigation had reached a dead-end. At least until Deirdre returned home to let them in to look around the place, or when either one of them would come up with a new and bright idea to work with. In the meanwhile, though, without a legitimate or legal way of gaining access to the building, Sam had taken to tinkering with his transphasic probe to try to get a reading from the outside. It wasn't going well.

'Do you think, if we asked nicely, Simon would let us hop over the fence into Deirdre's back garden?' he asked idly. He was knelt beneath the front window, crouching over a flowerbed and waving the wand along the windowsill, trying to spot any variances in the Akashic frequency. So far, there was nothing.

'I doubt it,' Alice answered, glancing over her shoulder at him. The suburban street may have been quiet enough for them to work uninterrupted, without having to worry about being accosted by anyone, but nonetheless Alice sat on the front wall keeping a lookout just in case. If anyone were to spot them, she could think of very few answers which would excuse their loitering. There is a certain threshold for what can be considered suspicious behaviour, and Sam Hain suspiciously lurking in a flowerbed under the window of an old woman's house crossed it. As did asking to go through someone else's house to vault over the fence. 'You can ask him if you really want to, though.'

Sam thought for a moment, genuinely considering the prospect for a brief second, before dismissing the idea with a hand-wave. 'Nah.' He returned to waving the TechnoWand along the length of the window as he tried to peer in, but he couldn't glimpse much beyond the net curtains. Occasionally, the wand would flicker with a dim white glow, but only for a moment. 'It's odd,' he said, continuing to state his thoughts out loud, 'this place should be saturated in magickal energy, but it's like the vase... There's a trace of something, but nowhere near as prominent as I'd expect.'

'Maybe the magick is just wearing off?'

'I doubt it. For a moment it looked like it was

leaking through into Simon's place, but even that waned. I'm honestly a little bit stumped.' He stood up from crouching in the flowerbed, and looked up at the red-brick building in front of him. 'The only thing I can think of now is to get inside somehow, and see if we can find out anything more.'

'You know,' Alice said with a sigh, 'it's moments like this, when I'm not sure what to suggest, and even you can't come up with a ludicrous idea which somehow weirdly works... I just wish things could be a little easier. Like maybe a hint to point us in the right direction, or a big flashing neon sign with the words "This Is The Answer."'

No big flashing neon sign with the words "This Is The Answer" appeared, but still it seemed as if Alice's wish had been answered. From somewhere along the street, they could hear the sound of shouting. They both turned to face the direction of the sound. The shout came again, and it almost certainly sounded like someone shrieking the word "help."

As they kept their eyes trained on the street, staring down the road to try and determine precisely where the voice was coming from, the shape of a young boy came into view. There was something unusual about him. It wasn't the fact that the boy wasn't the one who was crying for help – although it sounded as if the voice was coming from somewhere very close to him – it was the fact that he was soaring, quite contentedly, in the sky above one of the houses. The shouts, presumably, were coming from his suddenly – and quite rightly – distressed mother.

'Correct me if I'm wrong,' Sam said, squinting as he looked up into the blue sky and at the child floating around in it, 'but children don't spend much time in the sky, do they?'

'No,' Alice replied, equally as transfixed and bemused by the sight, 'no they do not.'

Kicking the dirt from the flowerbed off of his boots, Sam marched out of the garden gate and down the road, towards the house from which the cries for help were coming. Towards the flying child. 'Seems something stranger is afoot after all.'

'Hello?' Sam called out as they reached the house. It stood towards the end of one of the terraces, mercifully giving them a path up the side of the property towards the back garden. The back garden above which a young boy was performing loop-de-loops. 'Hello?' he said again, raising his voice at the side gate. 'It's come to our attention that your child has inexplicably learned to fly.'

'We might be able to help,' Alice added.

'I don't know,' the occult detective said, lowering his voice, 'I've never had to fish a child out of the sky. Depending on what magick has caused this, I'm not sure how easily – or safely, for that matter – we'll be able to get him down.' He noted the admonishing look on Alice's face. 'I didn't say we wouldn't. I just... Haven't got a handle on what's going on yet.'

The gate swung open, revealing a particularly frantic-looking woman. Her eyes darted wildly between her two unexpected visitors. Evidently today was the kind of day for sudden and unexpected things. 'Thank god you're here,' she breathed, although she had no idea who either of them were. She simply seemed grateful to not be contending with the problem on her own. 'Timmy was jumping on the trampoline, but after a few bounces he just... He didn't come back down.'

She ushered Sam and Alice through the gate and into the garden. It was a fairly nice garden. The edges were lined with bright flowerbeds and small plants, and a well-kept potting shed stood at the far end next to a tall tree. A new-looking barbecue sat on the patio, with an arrangement of garden furniture positioned around it. A child's trampoline sat in the middle of the neatly kept lawn, with a couple of water guns laying by the side of it. The one thing notably wrong about the garden was that Timmy was decidedly no longer in it, although his shadow continued to dance in patterns on the ground beneath him.

'How did this happen?' Alice asked, and immediately regretted the question. She very much doubted that Timmy's mother would have an answer for it. It was the kind of situation for which answers were very thin on the ground. Rather thin in the air, too.

'Where did you get the trampoline? Did you buy it from a mysterious travelling salesman, perhaps?' Sam enquired. Even if his question was decidedly stupider than Alice's, he didn't seem aware of it.

'No,' said the woman (who, despite having made no formal introductions, will be referred to as Judith forthwith, for the sake of narrative ease), looking at them both with an incredulous expression. She gestured frantically at the sky, and her son soaring in it. 'You think I have any idea why this would happen?' She made a noise somewhere between a snarl of frustration and a whimper of worry. 'It's like some kind of magic, or a curse.'

'Oh really,' Sam said, tilting his head ever-so-slightly, 'what was your first clue?'

Judith ignored him. 'I bet it was that bloody thing,' she said.

'What bloody thing?' Alice asked, standing by the side of Judith and looking up at Timmy. Although his mother was worried, he seemed quite happy about the whole situation. Flying seemed to be quite a joy for the boy.

'Oh, it was this... thing...' She was clearly agitated, preoccupied with her son flying overhead, and tried to mime the shape of the thing. She cupped her hands around an invisible base, and furiously waved a hand up and down an invisible stem. 'Like this vase kind of thing. It was out on someone's garden wall, just up the road.'

Alice already knew what both she and Sam thought of the vase, but she was intrigued that Judith apparently suspected something about it too. She was curious about what connection this woman thought linked the ornament and her flying son. 'What do you think the vase has to do with anything?'

'We were walking down the road yesterday, and Tim picked this vase up. I told him not to because it was someone else's. And it was right next to the bins, so I made him wash his hands when we got home. But I... This is going to sound mad, please don't think I'm being hysterical just because my kid is flying fifteen feet above the ground.'

'Trust me,' Sam said, 'things that seem utterly mad or unusual are our speciality.'

'A little bit later, last night, I found Tim suddenly had this mound of chocolate on his bed, so I asked him where he got it all from. He said the genie gave it to him. I mean, I didn't believe a word of it then, but now...' She looked up to the sky, where Timmy soared gracefully through the air, and a look of confused consternation washed across her face. 'Now I don't think he was making it up at all. I can hardly believe I'm saying this. I'd think it all utter nonsense if I hadn't seen Tim start flying, but... Could it actually be possible that vase *was* magic, and we've – this is stupid – and we've somehow released a genie? If there really are such things?'

Sam clapped his hands together. If he was the kind of man to jump and click his heels together, he probably would have done that too. 'Aha!' he suddenly exclaimed, startling both Alice and Judith. 'That's it!' His tone sounded more joyous and excited than was probably appropriate, considering a child could suddenly stop flying and fall a considerable distance to the ground.

'What's "it"?' Judith asked, whirling around to

face Sam with an almost accusatory expression. From somewhere above them, Timmy made a wooping sound. 'How is my son stuck in the air?'

'The genie. That's it,' Sam said, containing his enthusiasm and adopting a more "professional" demeanour. Not that he was particularly adept at anything resembling professionalism. 'Your son's not stuck in the air, he wants to be up there.' He looked up at the boy in the sky, who was now flying in a figure of eight, flapping his arms like an ungraceful bird. 'Don't you, Timmy?' he called up to him.

'Yeah,' Timmy shouted back down to them.

'See, he's quite happy up there.'

'That's not the bloody point, though, is it?' Judith's nostrils flared. 'What if he suddenly falls? Or even worse, what if he flies up even higher and can't come back down? Or finds himself in a jet's flight path?'

'All right, point taken,' Sam said, 'although I don't think you'll have to worry about that. If we're dealing with a djinn – a genie – and not a curse, then Timmy's just had a wish fulfilled.'

'Wait, what's this about a curse?' Judith asked, her eyes now filled with an all new fear.

'Nothing to worry about now,' he said.

Alice stepped up to the base of the trampoline, gazing up at the boy happily flying about. It didn't seem to concern him that his mother was evidently more than a little bit scared, and now two strangers were in his garden. 'That looks like a lot of fun, Timmy,' she called up to him, 'did you wish you could fly?'

'Yeah,' Timmy replied again, spinning around and swooping down, 'I was jumping. And jumping and jumping. And I saw some birds, so I wished I could fly too. I never want to come back down!' He soared back up into the sky, to a worrying height.

'That could be a bit of a problem,' Sam admitted, scratching his head. 'He can't stay in the sky forever.'

'Oh really,' Judith snapped back, 'you think?'

'I might be able to help, though,' he said, although it seemed like he was thinking out loud more than trying to reassure Judith. 'It'll be only temporary, and we'll have to coax little Timmy out of the sky for a moment, but it'll keep him safely on the ground until we've – quite literally – put the genie back in the bottle.'

'What's your plan, then?' Alice asked, turning to face Sam. 'You know how to deal with a genie?'

'Not precisely,' he said, 'but I do have an idea. Djinn are honourable beings. Powerful trickster spirits, and you really don't want to get on their bad side, but they always fulfil their side of a bargain. When a sorcerer conjures a djinn, they often make a deal or a pact of some kind; the djinn will fulfil the conjurer's wishes in exchange for something, favours or offerings. Although, a sorcerer can also trap a djinn, bind it to an object, and the djinn is duty-bound to obey whomsoever possesses its vessel.'

He snapped his fingers as another realisation hit him. 'That's what the symbol on the cap was for, to bind and seal the djinn! Anyway, traditionally each holder is usually granted three wishes. It's like using magick to manifest your will, but using a powerful being for quick and easy results. After which, the djinn must be commanded back into its vessel. In this case, the vase.'

'Jesus, you people are being serious about all this, aren't you?' Judith murmured, a slight quiver to her voice and a haunted look in her eyes. She could barely keep up with what Sam was wittering on about, let alone begin to fathom this fairytale she and Timmy now found themselves caught up in. Although it was less of a fairytale, more like a nightmare for her. She began to rub her temples. 'This is madness,' she breathed, sounding quiet and distant, talking more to herself than the others, 'this is utter, bloody madness.'

Sam had started to pace, seemingly in a world of his own as he reeled off his stream of consciousness. He trudged in a circle around the trampoline, stroking his chin contemplatively. 'Anyone who has come into contact with that vase would have been granted three wishes. We just need someone to make their last wish, and command the djinn back into the vase, and seal it shut. If it isn't commanded back into its vessel, well... It's best not to imagine what could happen when a powerful djinn is released from centuries of captivity with no one to control it.'

For a brief moment, Alice imagined it. The more one thinks of the potential problems of a rogue, possibly vengeful, genie, the more chaotic the possibilities become. 'Shit,' she said, 'I see what you mean. We'd better get the vase from the shop, and get that thing back in there as soon as possible. And how do we know who has the power to command it back in anyway?'

'Well, Timmy here is definitely a candidate.' He pointed up at the small boy, who had attracted the attention of a particularly curious robin. 'Hence why we need a temporary solution, until we can get the vase to be able to seal it away properly. We don't want anything untoward happening in the meantime, and if we get caught up in someone else's wish, there's no telling what might happen.'

'Right, any solutions spring to mind?'

'We're going to have to try and guard ourselves against its magick, try and dilute the effects,' he said, stopping in his tracks and spinning around to face her. 'We're going to need a tonic.'

'You're going to deal with a djinn with... Some tonic?' Alice asked, an incredulous expression across her face. Sam Hain had said many absurd things before, but this idea sounded borderline ridiculous. 'Fancy a couple of slices of lemon with that?'

'Alice, I know you're being sarcastic, but actually, yes. Some citrus fruit could help. Lemons can be quite effective at warding off evil, plus they'll give the tonic a lovely refreshing zest.'

Standing to the side of their discussion, Judith blinked perplexedly at the two strangers in her garden. Her eyes darted from one to the other, trying to keep up with what they were saying. As if her son being stuck in the sky wasn't already weird enough. 'Excuse me,' she said, 'I haven't got a sodding clue what you're on about, or what's going on anymore, but does this mean you have a way to rescue Timmy?'

With a single, stoic nod, Sam offered Judith a reassuring smile. 'I think so, yes,' he said. 'You, Tim, and anyone else who might have a run-in with the djinn.'

'So how do we go about creating this tonic of yours?' Alice asked. She was still somewhat sceptical, and wondered if this was another one of those times when Sam was making everything up as he went along. But, she considered, at this point anything was worth a shot.

'Firstly, we'll need a tonic water base.'

'I have tonic water in the fridge,' Judith offered helpfully.

'Perfect. That's one part sorted,' he replied. 'We'll need some protective herbs. Or maybe even some essence of frankincense, much more potent for protection, invoking spells and dispelling unwanted magick.'

'Oh, I don't have any of that,' Judith added, less helpfully.

Patting down the pockets of his jacket, Sam retrieved a miniscule glass vial with a small drop of yellowish oil inside. He looked at Judith apologetically. 'I don't have much,' he admitted, and cast his glance towards Alice. She offered a resigning shrug in response. 'If it's mixed with some herbs, it should be potent enough. Back at the flat I have a particular blend a hedge-witch once gifted me. Shouldn't take me long to fetch it.

Alice, are you okay to hold the fort here? Make sure things don't go too terribly awry until I get back?'

'Sure, as you wish,' she said, as Sam was already making his way through the garden gate, 'knock yourself out.'

So he did.

Meanwhile, somewhere in Islington...

Derek and Clare were settling in for a romantic evening's meal. The table was set, the candles were lit, the wine was open and the linguine was cooking. Today marked their two year anniversary, and Derek had been preparing for this day for a while. He'd been thinking things over the past few months and, although he had found himself getting cold feet throughout this previous week, he had decided today was the day. He was going to ask Clare to marry him.

It was still early in the evening by the time the dinner was ready, the autumn sun slowly starting to set, casting a warm orange glow through the window and across the table. Derek and Clare sat gazing out of the window, their hands meeting across the table, their fingers entwined, taking in the romantic view of the sun shining above the suburban landscape. Candle light flickered, glistening in their eyes and reflecting off of the cutlery. They ate and drank, and talked and laughed. They shared stories about their days, how work had been, and reminisced about their two years together.

'You know, funny thing about that,' Derek said, swallowing his mouthful of linguine before swilling down a quick gulp of wine, 'looking back over our history together. It makes one really start to think about what the future might hold too, doesn't it?'

'Oh, does it now?' Clare asked, a knowing tone in her voice, leaning across the table and delicately taking his hand in hers. She smiled coyly at him.

'So, mister handsome philosopher, what ponderings and musings of the future do you want to share with me?'

Derek cleared his throat. He took another mouthful of wine. Maybe it was the couple of glasses of nero d'avola now swimming in his head, or the romantic mood lighting provided by flickering candles and the evening sunlight streaming through the window, or the delicious meal they had just shared together. Or maybe, just maybe, it was the fact he could not take his eyes off of her, and his heart skipped a beat every time she smiled, and he felt himself falling that little bit more in love with her every day. Whatever it was, he knew that now was the time.

'Well, let's see...' he began, gazing lovingly into Clare's eyes. With the tips of his fingers, he started to trace tickling patterns along the lines and creases of her palm. 'I see us, together, for a long, long time ahead.'

'So you're a psychic now?' Clare giggled.

'Not psychic, just an optimist.' He smiled at her, and continued. 'I see happiness, and laughter, and even through the hardest times I see us helping pick each other up and keep one another going. I see many adventures we'll share together. I see us, older – but not necessarily wiser – in a nice, family home-'

'I like this,' she sighed, her fingers now playing with his as he talked. 'Keep going.'

'I hear children playing in the other room-'

'Wait, wait,' Clare held up her hand, a worried look on her face. 'Are they our children? Or did we kidnap them?' She gasped, dramatically holding her hands to either side of her face. 'Or are they the ghosts of two Victorian children who died in that house?'

'No ghosts, no kidnapping either,' Derek laughed, 'it's all quite above board. They're our children, honestly produced, the fruits of our labour.'

'Oh, that's a relief,' she said, comically wiping her brow, 'I was worried we'd moved into a haunted house. And I think you'll find it'll be the fruits of *my* labour, unless you want to give birth to save me the effort?'

'We'll cross that bridge when we come to it.' He grinned. 'Anyway, before we get to that part, I wanted to ask you something-'

Before he had a chance to say any more, the pattering of paws came rushing towards them. Through the doorway, his labrador, Rufus, came bounding in to them. Almost as swiftly as Rufus had arrived, Clare had got down from the chair and was on her hands and knees with the dog. She vigorously stroked his sides, ruffling his ears, while Rufus excitedly bounced around her. 'Who's a big beautiful floof? You are! Yes you are,' she fawned over Rufus, who was loving every minute of stealing the limelight.

'You know, I wish you would give me the same love and affection you give that dog!' Derek said, jokingly, and took a sip of his wine.

It was as if something changed in Clare in that moment. Her focus moved away from Rufus, who was happily rolling around on his back, and she looked at Derek with wide and adoring eyes. She grinned broadly and hurried over to him, ruffling his hair. Derek made a contented hum; he enjoyed the sensation of her fingers running through his hair. The thing that snapped him out of it was when she pinched both of his cheeks, her face close to his, while cooing 'who's a good boy?'

Playfully batting her hands away from his face, Derek laughed. 'Oh stop it,' he said with a smile. It was one of the many things he loved about her; her unashamedly silly sense of humour. It was cute. 'You know I think you're adorable, and that's what I wanted to-'

Again he found Clare cutting him off. Had he not known any better, he would've thought she was trying to avoid the conversation. Instead, she just seemed much more committed to the dog thing. 'Would you like a biscuit?' she asked in a cartoonishly high voice, still addressing him as if he was a lovable labrador.

'Har-dee-har,' he said, his voice taking on a more serious monotone, 'very funny. But there is something I wanted to talk with you about. Sensibly. Well, more of an important question I wanted to ask you.' He reached his hand out to take hers.

'Shakies?' Clare beamed at him, holding out her hand in turn. 'Shake!' Confusedly, Derek took her hand in his, and they shook. 'Good boy,' she cooed once more, 'you deserve a little treaty.' She turned, and started to make her way towards the kitchen; presumably to fetch Derek a biscuit. If she was really going to commit to this bit, he sincerely hoped she returned with a Hobnob instead of an actual dog biscuit.

He leaned back in the chair, tipping it ever so slightly as he reached towards the kitchen doorway behind him. 'Clare, babe,' he said imploringly, his arms outstretched to her, 'please, you know I love playing around, but I do need to talk with you.'

'I know what you want,' she said, her voice sounding a little lower and closer to her normal tone. Standing behind Derek, she slowly and gently wrapped her arms under his and around his waist. He leaned back to kiss her cheek. 'Ooh, someone wants a belly rub!' she squealed, and excitedly began to tickle her fingers across his stomach. 'Big full belly,' she playfully growled, lightly squeezing him where he was slightly doughier than he personally preferred, 'someone's already had more than a few treats. Yes he has!'

This was the final straw for Derek. He pushed her hands off of him, and stood up with such force that he knocked the chair over backwards. Wine spilled across the pristine table cloth. 'Jesus Christ, Clare!' he shouted, his agitation palpable, fixing her with a stern stare. 'I have my heart on my sleeve here for you, and you're pissing about. What the hell are you thinking?'

Having leapt back the moment he whirled around, Clare stood in the doorway to the kitchen. She folded her arms and furrowed her brow. 'Bad dog,' she pouted, wagging an admonishing finger at him, 'very bad dog.'

'I have no idea what's gotten into you,' he huffed, 'I just wanted to have a nice, quiet, romantic evening, and I had something important to ask you. But the minute I bring it up, you start doing... *This*! This is ludicrous, Clare.'

Reaching around the corner of the kitchen door, Clare retrieved a small spray bottle. In one swift motion, like a gunslinger in a Wild West movie, she aimed the bottle at Derek's face and doused him in several liberal squirts of cold water. 'Calm down, boy,' she commanded.

'You know what?' Derek sighed heavily, water trickling down his face and dripping from his nose. He reached for one of the napkins, mopping down his face and throwing the fabric dramatically back onto the table. 'Fuck this, I'm off.' As he made his way frustratedly towards the front door, he added, 'Let me know when you're ready to talk sensibly.'

'No!' Clare cried out the moment Derek began to walk down the stairs, and for a brief moment he hoped she was about to call him back. He paused on the steps, waiting for whatever she was about to say. 'No, no walkies now. We're staying in.'

With a sigh, Derek sombrely and laboriously continued down the steps and out of the door.

CHAPTER V

Everything happened all at once.

No sooner had Sam walked through the gate than he gripped the fencepost, firmly with both hands, and slammed his head against it. Hard. He stumbled, staggering backwards, eyeing the post with surprise and confusion. The same surprise and confusion with which Alice and Judith had watched him headbutt a post. Before either of them had had a chance to react, Sam's legs crumpled, he toppled to one side, and fell to the floor. Quite ungracefully, and very unconsciously.

His hat rolled across the path, forlorn and alone.

They wished this had been the only alarming thing to happen. Unfortunately, this particular wish remained unfulfilled. Nearby, from what sounded like a couple of houses along, there came a sudden cry of alarm, shortly followed by the distinct metallic clattering of coins. A lot of coins. 'Oh my good god,' a man's voice shouted, 'Sheila! Get a bucket!'

As she rushed to Sam's aid, Alice craned her neck to cast a glance behind her, only to see a thick cloud of what appeared to be an inordinate amount of coins raining down into one of the neighbouring gardens. 'What the fuck is happening...?'

Kneeling down beside the unconscious form of Sam Hain, Alice lightly tapped the side of his face. 'Are you secretly some kind of arbiter for reality or something?' she asked, although he was very unlikely to offer her any answer in his current state. 'The minute you fall unconscious, it's like the world gets even more bloody bonkers.' Other than a faint, disgruntled moan, Sam offered little in the way of a reply.

'I'll get him an ice pack or something,' Judith said, and she started to make her way towards the house. She hesitated, reluctant to be too far from her son. Taking a few hurried and panicked steps at a time, Judith would intermittently pause and take a cautionary look up to the sky. 'Keep an eye on him until I get back,' she said, flailing her hand in the direction of Timmy, 'just in case.'

Alice nodded, and looked up at Timmy in the sky. He seemed all right, flying about without a care in the world, and with little interest for what was going on on the ground below. Hastily, Judith scurried into the house. She emerged a few short moments later, brandishing a bag of frozen peas.

'Here we are,' she said, handing Alice the ice-cold bag of peas, although her eyes immediately darted up to watch her son.

'Thank you,' she said, and delicately placed the bag across Sam's forehead. 'Just wake up, you stubborn git,' she pleaded with him, 'what'd you knock yourself out for?'

The words echoed uncomfortably in her mind. *Knock yourself out.* Looking at Sam's unconscious face, his mouth slightly open and a trickle of drool gently oozing from his lips, the idea dawned on her. *No, it can't be, can it?* She was still coming to terms with the idea that they were now dealing with a genie, and not a curse as she had first suspected.

Up until they'd discovered the boy in the sky, nothing they knew of the case seemed much like wish-fulfilment; the testimonies from Deirdre and Simon were more akin to cruel misfortune, or even punishment. The idea that anyone could have wished these things to happen was unthinkable. But, now she found herself considering how her own turn of phrase seemed to have led to this moment, she wondered how much of the "curse" so far had been brought about by a poor choice of words.

She thought back to that morning, to when Deirdre Roberts had returned the vase and Alice had taken it from her. She remembered holding the vase, running her fingers along the detailing, and trying to fix the cap back into place. *Well-bloody-done*, her thoughts sarcastically congratulated her, *you touched an enchanted item, and now you're lumped with a genie with a cruel sense of humour.*

That was the thing, of course. She had unwittingly invoked the djinn – as had Deirdre, Terry, Timmy – and unknowingly wished things into reality. But, Alice thought, she now knew what they were dealing with. And, more to the point, she knew she held the power of the djinn to grant her wishes. She may have accidentally caused Sam to knock himself out, but she could also undo it.

'I wish Sam was fully conscious again,' she declared, and watched Sam's face with eager anticipation. She could feel each and every second ticking by as she waited, staring at him expectantly. Nothing happened. *Maybe it's all in the phrasing,* she considered, and tried again. 'I wish Sam was no longer unconscious.' She gave him a gentle nudge, hoping to kick-start him into coming round, but still he remained motionless, his eyes shut, and decidedly unresponsive. *Why didn't it work?*

Craning her neck around, she looked up to the boy in the sky. If, for whatever reason, she couldn't make Sam come round, maybe she could make Timmy come down. 'I wish Timmy was safely back on solid ground,' she said at first, but defiantly Timmy remained in the sky, flying around above the garden. 'I wish Timmy wasn't flying anymore,' she rephrased, although this one felt a little more risky. If it worked, she prayed they'd be able to catch the boy before he hit the ground. Not that she needed to worry. She wasn't sure whether to be grateful or frustrated when that wish didn't work either. *I must've somehow already used up my three wishes without realising it.* 'Shit.'

'Genie,' she called to the spirit, in the hope that it would be listening. 'I command you to return to your vase, and leave these people be.' It came as little surprise to her that, yet again, nothing happened. *Worth a shot...*

Alice's mind began to race. With Sam out of

action, Timmy still in the sky, a money monsoon not a few houses along, no wishes for an easy solution, but with a djinn still very much at large, she knew she would have to do something. Somehow, she intended to find a way to put things right. Or, at the very least, do her best to keep things from getting worse. *Well*, she thought, *if you're not going to be able to get the herbs from your flat, Sam, looks like I'll have to try and brew this tonic myself.*

Patting down the occult detective's motionless body, she searched for the small vial of frankincense. It took a while to find the right pocket, as apparently Sam wanted to make the most of every space available. There were, of course, the usual items – wallet, phone, keys, a pen and notebook – but in amongst these were a few decidedly stranger objects. The TechnoWand, a small collection of differently coloured crystals, a piece of chalk, a silver token engraved with a pentacle and several obscure symbols and, lastly, the vial. She took it out, examining the small amount of the yellowy oil. It would have to do.

'Liss?' Sam's voice groaned. His eyes slowly opened, as if his eyelids were heavily weighted. 'Wuh happ'n'd?'

'Oh thank goodness,' she breathed at the sight of him coming around. 'You had a bit of an altercation with a fencepost. How're you feeling?'

'Bassard ne'er saw it comin',' he slurred, and smacked his lips as if trying to dispel an unpleasant taste in his mouth. With a clumsy and uncoordinated hand, he batted at the air around her, before resting a limp and heavy hand on her arm. 'You gotta do thuh fing.'

'The thing?'

Sam's eyes scrunched up tight as he attempted to focus his thoughts. They were there, somewhere, floating in the peripheries of his consciousness, though they remained jumbled and elusive. His hand flapped about as he frustratedly tried to communicate his thoughts. 'Y'know, the thing wizza stuff.'

'Abundantly clear as ever,' she laughed, more relieved by the fact that he was at least semi-conscious. 'You mean the tonic?'

'Thassa-one,' he said, a sleepy smile softly curling his lips. 'Use m'bottle. S'good, will make potion... Portent?'

'I've got that,' she said, holding the vial up, 'the frankincense. It'll make the potion potent. What else do I need to do?'

With a quiet moan, Sam's eyelids fluttered. 'You know stuff,' was all he said before he lapsed out of lucidity again.

Bloody useful, her thoughts moaned, *what stuff?* The only stuff she knew was that they needed a tonic, to use some lemons and frankincense, and... *Herbs.* She recalled the book on witchcraft she had been reading earlier that day. Although there was nothing specifically about djinn dispersals – not that she remembered seeing, anyway – there were a couple of chapters dedicated to protection spells. Many of which involved the consumption, bathing in or burning of different herbs. With any luck, she thought, she might be able to concoct a tonic of her own. 'Do you have any herbs and spices in the kitchen, by any chance?' Alice asked, glancing over her shoulder at Judith.

'I might have some in the cupboard,' Judith said. She stood resolutely by the trampoline, looking up at her sky-borne son with worry. 'Mind you, I don't have any eye of newt or anything particularly witchy, or whatever it is you people are,' she added, turning to face Alice, almost tripping over in the process. Judith hadn't quite taken her eyes off of Timmy, and failed to notice the water gun laying at her feet. She caught her balance, and gave the toy a swift and scolding kick. This gave Alice her second idea.

'Thank you,' she said with a nod, 'if it's okay with you, then, I need to try and make this tonic.'

'Uh-huh,' came Judith's answer. She didn't seem to be paying much attention; Timmy had flown himself up higher into the sky, and his mother was naturally much more preoccupied with that. Alice took that as enough of a confirmation, and decided to see what options Judith's kitchen could offer her.

'Alice!' Sam exclaimed, slipping back into a more conscious state again. 'You gotta do the thing.'

'I know,' she smiled patiently at him, 'we've been over this. I'm on it.'

'Oh,' he droned, 'good.' Staring blankly up at the sky, his brow began to furrow. 'Why's this bed hard?'

With an amused sigh, she hooked her arm around him and gently tried to ease him up. 'It's a concrete path, Sam,' she said as she propped him up into a sitting position. He clutched the bag of frozen peas to his forehead, the frost starting to melt and gradually drip down his face. 'Let's get you somewhere more comfortable, shall we?'

'Yes please.'

She helped him up off of the ground, wrapping one arm around his waist and draping his around her shoulders to keep him steady. It took a bit of effort; he was heavier than he looked, not exactly helped by the fact that he wasn't supporting his own weight. His feet were unsteady, his legs flopping and uncoordinated, like a baby deer learning to walk. Together, they awkwardly waddled towards the patio furniture, Sam's legs almost performing a very lacklustre rendition of Riverdance beneath him, while Alice attempted to carry him forwards.

With an ungraceful heave, she flopped Sam down into one of the garden chairs. 'I'll be back in a minute,' she said, dashing over to grab one of the water guns from the lawn, before making her way in through the patio doors.

'Hey, thingy... Lady,' Sam called over to the woman who was worriedly watching her son in the sky.

'My name's Judith,' said Judith.

'Judith,' he repeated politely. 'Why's there now two of him up there?'

Meanwhile, elsewhere in Highbury, things had taken a turn for the weird.

Down the road, around the corner, and on the

pavement running alongside Highbury Fields, Inaya was about to receive some surprising good news. 'You're kidding me?' she exclaimed excitedly down the phone. 'Where did you hear this?'

'Well, I overheard some of the managers talking earlier today,' Jay began to explain. He and Inaya had been close ever since they first met on induction day at the office. After the former head of HR had resigned, the company were looking to fill the role, and – after some persuasion from Jay – Inaya had put herself forward for the position. 'According to Mike, it sounds like you are an absolute shoe-in!'

'You're serious, aren't you?' she asked, not quite believing him. She wanted the position, naturally – upward mobility, better career prospects, a decidedly comfortable pay-rise – but she never considered that she would actually get it. It was a lot to try and take in.

'I wanted to be the first to congratulate you on your imminent promotion.'

'Thank you!' she beamed. 'I don't think I'll quite believe it until I hear it straight from the horse's mouth, though.'

'It's true, you know,' an unexpectedly deep voice interrupted the phone call. Inaya had her head down, and hadn't noticed anyone was approaching her. She looked up to face the voice, and immediately leapt back in alarm. There, standing in front of her, was a horse.

This came as a surprise to Inaya for a number of reasons. Firstly, she had never seen a horse around Highbury Fields before. Secondly, she hadn't even seen this particular horse before it spoke; horses are rather large creatures, and she was sure she would've noticed the clip-clopping of hooves or, indeed, the sizeable equestrian walking down the road. Thirdly – and, quite possibly, most surprisingly – was the fact that the horse was speaking.

For a moment, Inaya struggled to form words. Her mouth gawped, opening and closing uselessly, looking like a shocked goldfish, as her brain played catch-up with reality. 'Jay?' she eventually uttered, 'I'm going to have to call you back.'

'Michael put in a good word for you,' the horse continued, 'he recommended you highly for the HR position.' The only thing which was more surprising than a well-spoken horse in the middle of Highbury, who had seemingly appeared out of thin air, was the fact that the horse seemed to have intimate knowledge of the managerial decisions of her office. And it was very keen to inform her about it.

She tried not to look the horse in the mouth. This was largely due to the fact that its lips moved in a most unsettling fashion when it spoke, and the situation was already disquieting enough as it was. But she may also have been confusing her idioms.

Back at Judith's residence, Alice was frantically rummaging through the kitchen. She opened cupboard after cupboard, looking through each of the cabinets for anything she could use for a protection spell. So far, she had found where

Judith kept the crockery, the pots and pans, and a small, miss-matched stock of non-perishable foods. Eventually, above the cooker, she discovered a cabinet stocked with a modest array of herbs and spices.

With her phone in one hand, she began rifling through the ebook's pages for protection spells. She had tried searching for the keyword "djinn," and the book did have a recommendation, albeit a not particularly convenient one. It suggested burning benzoin and wormwood for protection from, and to banish, malicious djinn and other malignant spirits. Alice doubted Judith would have either of those, let alone both. She wondered if that might be similar to what Sam was planning to get from his flat, before she unwittingly caused him to knock himself out.

She continued hurriedly flicking through the pages, looking for a spell which used some slightly more readily-available ingredients. She was sure she had seen some which were much more easy to come by. Page after page flashed by as her thumb swiped rapidly across the screen. Some spells took more effort to conjure than she had time for, others felt too simple and "wishy-washy" to be potent enough for the circumstances.

There was a spell of protection by bathing in fresh basil leaves, there was a magickal barrier created by placing bay leaves in the corners of a room, and there was a charm for warding off vampires with garlic and peppermint. None of which struck her as being particularly useful in the present situation.

There was even a method for trapping a genie in a bottle, which Alice almost missed as she hastily swiped by, and had to double back to read it. This, too, seemed to be relying on things being more benign, or at least a little bit normal. The book recommended leaving an open bottle out with some sweet food to tempt the genie in and seal it inside, like a cartoon character trying to catch a mouse.

'Sod it,' she muttered to herself, putting her phone away with annoyance, 'if I can't find what I need in you, I'll have to figure something out on my own.'

Although the spellbook hadn't offered up anything fitting for their present predicament, it hadn't been entirely unhelpful. Alice had noted the herbs most commonly used in protection spells; whether they be used in baths, or placed around the home, or placed in charm pouches, they all were used for their protective properties. And if these properties worked in particular practices, she reasoned, then they could be adapted. She glanced back up at the open herb and spice cabinet.

Much to her frustration, nothing in the cabinet was exactly spell-like. It was more of an assortment of ingredients to spice up a home-cooked meal. As far as she was aware, garam masala and curry powder very rarely cropped up in witchcraft. If push came to shove, though, she could use the Italian mixed herbs; it may have been mostly oregano and thyme, but there was a bit of basil in there, too. Basil seemed to appear in enough of the spells to purportedly have protective properties, so it was worth considering.

She put the jar of mixed herbs on the counter – just in case that was the best she could do – alongside the vial of frankincense and a pepper mill. Pepper, she had read, not only was used for protection magick to ward off malign spirits, but also served to amplify the properties of the other ingredients. Which, given how her search had been going so far, she thought was going to be sorely needed.

Opening the fridge, Alice retrieved the bottle of tonic water. Two lemons were already out, resting in a fruit bowl on the kitchen side, so at least those elements had come together easily. Although, at this point, she dejectedly felt like she was making a refreshing drink with a herby twist rather than a magickal tonic. It was just as she was about to close the fridge that Alice spotted something. Two somethings, in fact, looking leafy and green, tucked away on the side of one of the shelves. She picked up the bundle of leaves and grinned. *Fresh basil and bay leaves. Perfect!*

She wasted no time in preparing the concoction. She took a jug down from one of the cupboards, poured in the fizzling tonic water, and set about adding the ingredients. There was a rule of five with invoking protective magicks, and she was pleased to see she had assembled five key ingredients for the tonic. First, she dripped the last drops of Sam's frankincense oil to the water. A strange and pungent aroma rose from the liquid. It wasn't quite as citrussy as the resin she had smelled him burning before; instead, this was closer to unsweetened liquorice, with a faint undertone of something almost similar to menthol.

With the core and most potent ingredient in the tonic, Alice chopped up the basil and bay leaves into fine flakes. A fresh and herby smell lingered in the air as she scooped up a handful of the leaves and sprinkled them into the jug. Next, she sliced the lemons, cutting them into thin wedges and dropping them into the fizzing concoction. Lastly, she twisted the pepper mill, grinding fresh black pepper straight into the mixture. All that remained now was to activate the tonic and imbue it with magickal intent. *No small feat.*

Some of the spell recipes she had seen had been accompanied by incantations, short chants or mantras to recite to invoke the energies within. Although, as she was already going off book with this concoction, she couldn't refer to any precise wording for this particular potion. But, as Sam had once said to her many moons and several strange situations ago, "nine-tenths of magick is intent." She would just have to make it up as she went along. *Specific spell or not,* she told herself, *this will bloody well work.* It did little to assuage the anxious tension bubbling in her chest, though. Picking up a spoon and hovering it over the tonic, she closed her eyes and took a few deep, steadying breaths. *Focus. Here goes nothing.*

'Warding magick against this djinn,' Alice began to intone, slowly and methodically, thinking of the right words to say, 'protecting tonic charmed herein.' She felt the beat and rhythm of each word as she spoke. There was an indefinable sense of power and purpose to rhymes. Stirring the concoction in a clockwise direction, it began to hiss. She continued. 'I cast this spell to guard us from harm,' a brief pause as her mind rushed to find another rhyming word, 'that this genie's magick be disarmed. Wayward wishes be undone, dispersed with spray from this water gun.' With that, she gave the tonic five final stirs, and tapped the spoon five times on the lip of the jug.

The tonic bubbled and fizzed, charged with the magick she had spoken into being. Something felt different in Alice, too. She couldn't quite place her finger on what, but she could almost feel the intent and energy of her words emanating from her being and imbuing the tonic with their power. There was a peculiar sense of achievement. She was more than a little bit proud of the spell she had conjured on the spot, too. *This must be how Sam feels*, she thought as she looked at the jug of tonic in front of her, *working magick on the fly*.

She poured some of the tonic into a glass, and took a mouthful of the concoction herself. Alice grimaced. She already had her suspicions about what it might have tasted like, but nothing could've prepared her for the curious medley of flavours. It was a peculiar blend of liquorice and pepper, with herby notes and a twist of citrus, fizzy and strangely sharp. It wasn't unpleasant, more unexpected. If anything, she could imagine it being served as a cocktail in a bar in Shoreditch. Not that she was likely to order it if it was.

Unscrewing the cap of the water gun, Alice carefully poured the contents of the jug into the reservoir and sealed it shut. She held the toy weapon in her hands, and with a singular and purposeful thrust of the pump, Alice stepped out into the garden. *Lock and load.*

The early evening sun was still shining bright over the garden, and Timmy was still happily flying around in a figure of eight some fifteen or twenty feet above the ground. Judith remained decidedly unhappy about this last fact. She was almost beside herself, her fingers scrunching up in her hair as she stared, helpless, at her son soaring in the sky. The moment she heard the trundling sound of the patio door being slid across, accompanied by hurried footsteps across the patio, she whirled around to face Alice.

'Oh thank god,' she breathed, somewhere between exasperation and relief, 'please tell me you've figured something out. He still won't come down, and I don't know what to do. I-' she paused, her eyes darting to the water gun clutched in Alice's hands. She was wielding it as if it was a shotgun. Judith boggled, wholly confused and more than a little bit agitated at the sight. 'What the bloody hell are you expecting that to do?'

'This?' she said, raising the water gun and angling it upwards, pointing it in Timmy's direction. 'This will help get your son back down on to solid ground.' *I hope,* she added to herself.

Judith's arms flapped in useless exasperation at her side. 'Sure, why not,' she squeaked. 'My little boy is flying, and you're going to shoot him down. With a water pistol.'

'Unconventional,' came a groaning voice from the garden chair, 'but inventive.' Sam still appeared to be having trouble focusing, but he seemed a little bit brighter, more alert, than he had done before. A bag of soggy, half-defrosted peas sat on the table next to him.

'How're you feeling?' Alice asked him. She knew she had to get Timmy out of the sky as soon as possible, but she couldn't not make sure Sam was okay. Obviously "okay" may have been a bit of a stretch – he had still been in and out of consciousness only a few moments ago, after all – but at least not-worse.

His eyes squinted slightly as he looked up at her and he made a discontented moaning sound. 'Like my head's been trampled by elephants.' He wasn't slurring his words any more, and had managed to formulate a sentence with a coherent simile, which was a good thing. 'Not two of everything any more, though. More like watching a 3D movie without the glasses.' He laughed, and immediately whined and winced as the mirth jostled his brain too much. 'You done the... Bollocks. The thing?'

'I've made the tonic, yes,' she said, 'it's a bit more of a home-brew than what you probably planned, but it's something.'

With his eyes closed, Sam slowly nodded. Despite his lucidity, he was barely back on form. 'Good,' he breathed.

'There's still some in a glass inside for you, see

if it helps clear your head, but first,' Alice said, patting the side of the water gun, 'I'm going to bring Timmy back to Earth.' She rested an affectionate hand on Sam's shoulder, and made her way into the middle of the garden. If she positioned herself just right, and hit the correct angle, the water gun would have a decent enough range to get Timmy. She hoped.

Tilting her head to the side and closing one eye, Alice took aim. She lined up the shot, carefully trying to follow Timmy's flight path. Every now and again, he would suddenly loop or swoop, spinning around in the air and change direction, but he mostly seemed content gently drifting for the moment. Just as the boy was about to line up with the nozzle of the gun, Alice pulled the trigger.

A short, impotent stream of water spurted and sputtered from the nozzle, shooting a slightly foamy spray no more than a couple of feet ahead. 'Tits,' Alice hissed, gripping the pump and vigorously thrusting it back and forth. 'Needs more pressure.'

'It might need more pressure,' Sam said helpfully from behind her.

'Got it, thank you,' she called back to him as she continued to pump the water gun. The moment she could feel the pressure building up to the point she couldn't pump it any more, she took aim again.

This time, the stream of water achieved a much greater range. It fired in a near-perfect straight line, angled upwards, for a good twenty feet before it sharply curved back down to the ground. Timmy watched with amusement as the stream of water narrowly missed him, shooting past just ahead of him, and he spun around to look at Alice.

'Missed me!' he laughed and swooped down, hovering a little closer to the ground. 'Bet you can't get me,' he taunted her.

'Bet I can,' she playfully shouted back, before adding beneath her breath, 'third time lucky...'

'Don't play games with him,' Judith instructed as she watched on with bewilderment and utter panic. 'Just get him down safely.'

'Don't worry,' Alice replied, trying to sound reassuring, although her focus was entirely on making the next shot count, 'he'll be safe and sound on the ground soon.' She carefully lined up the water gun. It was a little more difficult this time; Timmy was watching her with eager anticipation, excitedly moving this way and that to evade her. Attempting to catch him out, she pulled the trigger as she quickly swept the gun from left to right.

Judith felt as if her heart had leapt into her throat, before diving down into the pit of her stomach, as she watched her son perform a similar act of acrobatics in mid-air. He hadn't been expecting the sweeping shot, and propelled himself upwards and backwards to evade it, narrowly avoiding crashing into the tree at the end of the garden in the process.

'Missed again!' he mocked. Poking his tongue out, sticking his thumbs in his ears and waggling his fingers, he taunted them with a broad and cheeky grin across his face.

'Timothy!' his mother scolded. Her concern and anxiety had ramped up to a panicked anger. It was one thing fearing he might either fly too far, or suddenly fall to the ground; it was another now that he had nearly had a high-speed run in with a tree. 'This isn't a game. Stop pissing about and come down now, before you get hurt.'

Timmy, much like any other child who thought they had one-up on their parents, was not inclined to listen. 'I don't want to,' he laughed, hovering between the branches. What was she going to do about it, come up there and get him? She couldn't fly! As if to prove a point, he flew further up the tree, crashing through branches and leaves, twigs scraping and scratching against him as he shot up through the canopy.

'I really don't know if I'm going to hug him or ground him the minute he's safe,' Judith muttered to Alice, 'maybe both?'

'Let's just get him down before you decide whether to be relieved or annoyed,' she said, although she understood the sentiment. He may have been only a young child, but Alice was feeling more and more determined to get him with the water gun so he wouldn't be quite so smug about being able to fly away. And for his own safety, too, of course. 'I might have an idea. Just be ready to catch him with the trampoline.'

Nervously, Judith nodded, and she stood beside the trampoline. Alice took a few steps forwards, approaching the tree at the far end of the garden. 'That's not fair,' she called up to Timmy, as he hovered proudly above the canopy, 'how am I meant to reach you there? You're well out of range!' She waved the water gun in his direction. 'You know, I bet you couldn't fly down here and back up without me getting you.'

'I can, too!' Timmy yelled down to her.

'I don't know,' she said, loudly but dismissively, as she started to slowly walk away from him, 'you'd have to be really fast.'

'I can be very fast,' he shouted. Not one to turn down a challenge, especially not one which questioned his skills, he angled himself towards the ground. 'Watch!'

With a sudden rush of air, Timmy rocketed down from the treetop and flew towards the ground. He swooped low, only a few feet from the ground, as he glided alongside Alice. 'See?' he taunted, and started to arc his way back up into the sky, flapping his arms as he began to climb higher. Seizing this brief window of opportunity, with his back now to her and while still relatively close to the ground, Alice raised the water gun and fired. Her aim had been just ahead of his trajectory, and although the tip of the stream shot over his shoulder, the rest of the water hit its mark.

There came a wail of surprise and disappointment as Timmy felt the cool water splash against his neck and begin to unpleasantly trickle down his back. This was shortly followed by the much more unpleasant sensation of falling, and he shrieked as he felt himself rushing towards the ground like a stone. He flapped his arms in a desperate bid to stay in the air, but to no avail. He screamed.

'Oh Christ!' Judith exclaimed. Her knuckles were white as she gripped the frame of the trampoline tight. Rushing towards her falling son and trying to carry the ungainly shape of the trampoline with her, she threw herself forwards with arms outstretched, propelling the trampoline out beneath him. In that moment, she felt as if everything was playing out in slow motion.

Timmy plummeted down, landing just within the edge of the trampoline. He bounced once, he bounced twice, and he bounced thrice. Finally, he lay there on the taut fabric of the bounce pad, his eyes wide and in shock. From somewhere on the ground beside him, his mother breathed a loud sigh of relief. When she had pushed herself back up onto her feet, she threw her arms around her son in a tight embrace. 'Don't scare me like that again, alright?'

A light spattering of water drizzled them both as they embraced. There was the faint aroma of liquorice and pepper as they felt the cool droplets landing on their skin, in their hair, against their clothes. Judith twisted her head around to see Alice arcing the stream of the water gun to shower them both in the tonic. 'Do you mind?' she asked, an indignant look upon her face, and Alice obligingly lowered the gun.

'Nice shooting,' Sam said as Alice walked over to him. 'I assume. Everything's all blurry still.'

She pointed the water gun at him and pulled

the trigger. Sam scrunched his eyes tight, bracing for the spray of tonic. Except, it never came. Only the faint fizzling sound of the gun's nozzle foaming uselessly. Alice gave the gun an investigative shake. She heard the lumpy sound of the lemon slices bouncing inside the reservoir chamber, but it sounded suspiciously empty otherwise. It had been feeling progressively lighter, but she hadn't realised it was empty already.

'Wait there,' she said, holding a finger up to him, and she dashed inside the house.

'Trust me,' he said, resting his head heavily in his hands, 'I'm not inclined to move any time soon.'

Within moments, Alice emerged carrying a small glass tumbler. There was approximately a shot's worth of tonic water, with pieces of green herbs and a slice of lemon floating in it. 'Here,' she said, handing him the glass, 'have a drink of this.'

Taking a tentative and experimental sip of the tonic, Sam swilled the liquid around in his mouth. He pulled a face one might expect of a wine connoisseur tasting a fine vintage, and swallowed. 'Interesting,' he said, 'very interesting.' He smacked his lips as if trying to savour the curious taste. 'Tastes a bit more like a cleansing spell, with a hint of protection magick, and a twist of lemon.'

He rolled his eyes about, as if he was attempting to look around inside his own skull. 'And I think it's doing wonders for my concussion, too. My brain doesn't feel like its in a vice made of cotton wool quite as much.' With an approving nod, he added, 'Very nicely done. I'm impressed.'

Alice tried to hide her pride. Despite the stressful situation of trying to get a child out of the sky – who did everything he could to evade her help – she was still feeling overjoyed with not only crafting her own spell, but the fact that it had worked quite successfully too. The approval from the (debatably) expert opinion of Sam Hain was the cherry on top of this rather sumptuous cake. She felt a tremendous sense of accomplishment; not that she was one to blow her own horn, of course.

'All in a day's work,' she said as humbly as she could muster. 'I had to improvise, make do with what little was available, but I think it worked out okay.'

'I'll say,' he said, nodding towards Timmy, who was now jumping up and down on the trampoline, trying to get back in the sky. No matter how high he jumped, or how loudly he shouted he wished he could fly, he couldn't quite escape gravity. Either he'd used all three of his wishes, or Alice's charmed concoction had successfully severed his connection to the djinn completely. 'You got the boy back down to terra firma with just a few shots from a water gun. And,' Sam continued, gingerly lifting himself up from the garden chair and looking around, 'my head doesn't feel like it's going to explode. All in all, I'd call that quite the success.'

'Thank you,' she said, beaming at him, 'but let's not celebrate just yet. We've still got a djinn to deal with. Somehow.' Alice looked imploringly at him.

'Please tell me you've got some ideas in that refreshed mind of yours?'

Sam gazed up at the sky contemplatively. As the evening was beginning to wear on, the once blue sky was beginning to take on a faintly yellow hue. 'Well,' he began, 'no.'

'No?' she repeated, somewhat incredulously. 'No bright inspiration? I'd hoped your head would be full of fresh ideas now!'

'I think it's a bit like rebooting a computer,' he pondered, 'it might be running smoothly, but it still needs time to spool up again.' Suddenly, it was as if a light switch had been turned on inside Sam's head. His eyes widened, his eyebrows raised, and he snapped his fingers, pointing at Alice. 'Oh!' he exclaimed. 'You have wishes! That's why I... Y'know.' He gestured around the bump on his forehead. It had apparently taken him this long to realise why he had suddenly felt compelled to bang his head against a fencepost. The swelling was going down a little, at least.

Shaking her head regretfully, Alice said, 'No. Not any more. I think that was my last one, I haven't been able to wish anything to happen since.'

'Well, shit,' he groaned, 'I hope you wished for something good along the way.' Again, Alice shook her head. She wished she had; which was ironic, really. 'Tried commanding the djinn back into the vase?'

'Tried that too. I don't think it worked; it didn't make you any less concussed, and it was only the tonic which got Timmy back on the ground.' She looked up to the sky, an expression on her face as if she was trying to perceive something far away. 'It might sound strange, but I can still *feel* it around. Kind of like glimpsing something in the corner of your eye, just out of reach. And I know it's not listening to me.'

'Doesn't sound strange at all,' Sam said with a casual shrug. 'If it didn't go back to its vase, it's still going to be around here, lurking just outside of our perception.' It was strangely reassuring for Alice that whenever she found herself thinking something most people would consider weird, Sam treated it as an obvious fact. 'Which means one of two things,' he continued, 'either the djinn is still imprinted on someone yet to make their last wish, or it's been unshackled for so long that it's gone rogue. And I really bloody well hope it's the first one.'

'What about Terry?' Alice asked. 'Could the djinn still be bound to him? Maybe he disappeared before he could make his last wish. And with what we know now, perhaps we missed something.'

'Good thinking,' Sam said, clapping his hand on her shoulder. 'Seems like we need to pay another visit to Simon Melville, see if we can't resolve this before things get any more out of hand.'

As they prepared to leave, Judith came over to thank them both for their help. She didn't quite understand what had happened, or how Alice had done what she had done, but she didn't have to; she was just grateful that her son had been brought safely back down out of the sky. Timmy, on the other hand, seemed less grateful of this fact. Although he'd had fun while Alice was trying to shoot him, he wasn't keen on the fact he hadn't been able to take flight again.

With a final farewell, and a parting warning to not make any idle wishes on the off-chance they came true, Sam and Alice set off down the pathway, making their way back towards the Melville's residence.

'Well then,' Alice said, 'that's the end of that chapter.'

Chapter VI

Simon Melville answered the door much more curtly than he had done before. His face peered out through the narrow gap he had opened, eyeing Sam and Alice with a scrutinous and wary expression. 'Oh, it's you again.'

'Yes, us again,' Sam said cheerily, not taking heed of Simon's less than welcoming demeanour. 'Some new evidence has come to light which I suspect will help with your husband's case.'

'You're not with the police at all, are you?'

'What?' Sam hadn't expected to find himself on the back foot; he thought they'd be able to pick up where they'd left off. But evidently, things could never be quite that simple. He knew they'd had it far too easy just running into Judith, and the revelation of her djinn dilemma. The universe rarely remained so straightforward. 'I don't know— What?'

Simon fixed them both with a firm glare. 'I had an investigator turn up not long after the two of you left.' He looked them both up and down. Sam with his worn-looking black jacket and trousers, which appeared to have acquired grass stains since they'd last met, as well as what seemed to be a bruised bump on his forehead (he wasn't surprised; he had half a mind to strike this man, too). Alice in her creased jeans and denim jacket, who inexplicably now smelled faintly of liquorice and basil. 'Uniformed, I might add, with ID tags. So I'm left wondering, who the hell are you, and what do you want with me and my family?'

Clearing his throat, Sam knew there was very little point bluffing his way through another interaction. 'Well, I'm Sam Hain. I'm an occult detective. This is my friend and associate, Alice Carroll.'

'Hello,' Alice chimed in, offering a nervous smile and a quick wave. Most of Simon's indignation seemed primarily focused on Sam.

'We're not officially with the police, no, but we investigate and deal with matters that perhaps Scotland Yard would be ill-equipped to handle.'

'What does any of that even mean?' As he listened to Sam, Simon's face seemed to gradually be shifting away from indignation and into something resembling concerned confusion.

'It means our expertise goes beyond matters the Metropolitan Police couldn't even begin to understand.'

'We were investigating something else, which seems to be connected to you, and your husband's disappearance,' Alice added, 'it led us here.'

'So when you asked us if we had come about Terrence, and that you had been expecting detectives... Well, we weren't technically lying.'

For a moment, it seemed as if Simon was

contemplating what they had said. He pressed his forehead against the inside of the door frame, gazing down at the floor, and closed his eyes. A long, frustrated huff escaped from his lips. 'I wish you would just leave me alone,' Simon said.

'Okay, we'll leave you be,' Sam replied with a courteous nod. He turned on his heels and began to walk off down the pathway towards the road. For a moment, Alice watched him as he went, expecting him to turn around any second, but he didn't. The occult detective continued around the end of the path and along the pavement, heading off down the road.

'Excuse me for just one second,' she said to Simon, and hurried after Sam.

'Please, no need to be excused,' Simon replied exasperatedly.

Within a brief moment, Alice had caught up to Sam. 'Wait,' she beckoned to him, 'wait. Where are you going?'

Without turning to face her, Sam responded, 'What does it look like? The man said he wished for us to leave, so I'm leav-' He barely finished his sentence before he stopped in his tracks. 'Oh for bloody hell's sake! I hate genies,' the occult detective shouted, spinning around and racing back towards the door to the Melvilles' household.

'There we go.'

'The tonic must've been just strong enough to undo the magick, but evidently it's not a hundred-percent fool-proof,' he ranted as he marched himself back up the Melvilles' path.

'Well, you're living evidence of that,' Alice joked. Sam snorted, but didn't dignify the jab with a come-back.

Repeatedly thumping on the door, Sam tried to peer through the frosted glass for anyone the other side. Something which may or may not have been the indistinct and distorted shape of a man in a shirt seemed to be moving some way further back in the hall. Sam crouched down in front of the door, pushing his hand through the letter box, and pressed his face against it.

'Simon!' he called through the letterbox, 'I know you can hear me, so please just listen. We may not have been the investigators you were expecting, but I believe we are precisely who you need right now. I think we know how to help your husband, but you're going to have to trust us. Something far stranger than we originally suspected is afoot, and I'm not going to shout about it and disturb your neighbours.'

Turning away from the letterbox, Sam glanced over his shoulder to make sure no one was watching him. An older couple and their cocker spaniel were stood at the end of the pathway, staring curiously at the man squatting on the doorstep and shouting into a letterbox. Swiping at the air as if attacking a particularly persistent mosquito, Sam gestured for them to move on. 'Piss off,' he hissed.

'Now I've already drawn a small audience as it is,' he continued, returning to shout through the letterbox, 'and I really don't want to keep-' He didn't quite finish his sentence, as the letterbox swung away from him, taking his hand with it. Sam was yanked forwards, losing his balance from his squatting position on the doorstep, ungracefully trying to free his hand from the door and stand back up. As he pulled himself up, straightening the lapels of his jacket, he found himself standing face to face with Simon Melville. 'Thank you,' he said graciously.

'Okay, you've got my attention,' Simon intoned, his face rigid in a stern expression, 'even if it is just to get you to shut up.' His eyes darted to something just beyond Sam's left shoulder, and his face immediately softened, a broad and toothy smile stretched across his lips as he lifted his arm up and waved. 'Glen, Barbara,' he called out. Sam looked back over his shoulder and saw the couple walking their dog again, this time heading in the opposite direction, presumably having looped back around to watch. 'Can't stand them,' Simon hushed between gritted teeth, 'they're like vultures for neighbourhood gossip.' When the couple had carried on their way, and were safely out of earshot, he asked, 'So, what is it?'

'I know you're going to have a hard time believing this, so just bear with me a moment,' Sam began, his hands moving erratically as he began to explain, as if he was playing an invisible piano. 'I have reason to believe your husband may have invoked the powers of a genie, and it has somehow spirited him away.'

'Oh for heaven's sake,' Simon moaned, his eyes rolling with incredulity. 'Goodbye.' He swung the door, expecting it to slam shut in Sam's face, but instead it stopped just a few inches short with a dull thud. Looking down, Simon saw Sam's boot firmly placed over the threshold and propping the door open.

'You opened the door, you were willing to hear me out, you can't go back on that now,' Sam said, seemingly undeterred by having a door nearly slammed in his face. Even if he wasn't keen on the idea of a second concussion that day. 'All I ask is a few more moments of your time. Then you can kick us out, slam the door behind us, whatever, but I hope you'll at least let us try to help.'

Peering around Sam, Simon looked towards Alice. He had thought earlier on how she seemed the more amiable – or, more precisely, less irritating – of the two. As if answering his unspoken question, she sheepishly smiled at him and said, 'I know it's hard to believe, and it sounds incredibly far-fetched, but I genuinely believe we're onto something too. Please.'

With a reluctant sigh, Simon bowed his head. 'Very well. Come on in.' He pulled the door open again, wide enough to let the both of them through. 'Just don't make me regret this.'

'We won't,' Sam said, hastening his way inside. 'We might just need to speak with your children, if that's okay?'

'Not without me there,' Simon snapped, 'I don't want you disturbing them.' It was futile, though; Sam wasn't waiting for the answer. As Alice stepped through the door and began to follow Sam, Simon leaned in and spoke in a hushed tone. 'Is he always this obnoxiously irritating?'

'More often than not... Yeah.'

He offered little more than a tut and a disbelieving shake of his head as he closed the door behind them.

Outside on the street, Glen and Barbara and their spaniel walked past again, eyeing the front of the house with the utmost nosiness.

The smell of fresh cooking hung in the air, and the sound of two voices could be heard emanating from the lounge. As Sam and Alice stepped through the door into the living room, they were greeted by the curious faces of two children. Katie and Toby. They couldn't have been any older than eight and ten respectively, and both had stopped drawing the moment the two strangers had entered the room.

'Hello,' Sam said, awkwardly raising his hand to greet them both. The children simply stared at him uncertainly.

Stepping through the door just behind him, Alice beamed a smile at Toby and Katie. 'Hey,' she said, 'I'm Alice, and this is Sam. We know things have been a bit strange lately, and we were wondering if we could talk to you a little about it and what's happened to your dad. Can we come in?'

Katie leaned across the pieces of paper scattered about in front of them, adorned with pictures and scribbles, and whispered something into Toby's ear. He nodded, looked at her, looked up at Sam and Alice, and then whispered something into Katie's ear. With a decisive nod to one another, they turned to face the newcomers. 'You can,' Toby addressed them, 'would you like to draw with us too?'

Pushing his way past Sam and Alice, Simon made his way into the living room, carrying a cup of tea. In stark contravention of traditional British hospitality, he had not offered either of them any tea. Even though the kettle had only just boiled. 'Sorry, guys,' he said as he carefully stepped around the children, and slumped himself down in an armchair. Casting an uncertain stare towards Sam and Alice, he pointedly sipped his tea.

'Of course, we'd love to draw!' Alice grinned, and hurried her way around the sofa and sat down. Toby eagerly handed her a piece of paper and a couple of crayons. She wasn't terribly keen on his choice of colour palette for her – vivid tangerine, violet, and olive green – but she could work with it. 'What are we drawing?'

'Whatever you want!' Katie declared, triumphantly holding up her picture of what might have been a unicorn made of candyfloss.

'Very nice,' Alice politely lied. 'I might draw-' her mind raced for an idea, something she could conjure up out of her poor hand of crayons '-a flower.' She may have been lying about the niceness of Katie's drawing, but she was absolutely truthful about her excitement to draw.

Sam sat himself down beside her, helping himself to a handful of crayons too. He couldn't be considered a talented artist by any stretch of the imagination, but he could create a protection sigil to keep any unwanted paranormal activity at bay. He began by drawing a binding circle, and started to sketch esoteric symbols within it.

'Now, I hear things have been a bit unusual lately,' Alice said, keeping her focus on drawing the flowers. Although she was only working with crayons, she was quite pleased with the likeness of an iris she had drawn. 'Do you want to talk about it?'

Toby and Katie remained silent for a moment. They continued to draw across the paper, feverishly scribbling whatever vision had crossed their imaginations. Eventually, Katie made a "hmm" sound, and looked up at Alice. 'Well,' she said, pausing as if she was weighing up the most important events of the past few days. 'It's been okay. School was okay. It's strange now that Daddy Terry is different, though.'

'Different?' Alice pressed. She didn't want either Katie or Toby to feel like they were being interrogated, but she was hoping they'd be able to elaborate a little more. 'Daddy Simon told us that you said Daddy Terry seemed scared. Is that what you mean?'

The children giggled and laughed. 'No, no,' Toby said, his voice jumping with each chuckle, 'he wasn't scared of anything!' This seemed to be news to Simon, who leaned forward and listened intently to his children, his tea cup nestled in his hands.

'He even chased the monsters out from under my bed,' Katie added proudly. 'He's very brave, the things in the shadows are scary.'

Something sounding like a laugh rose from Sam. 'Tell me about it,' he said with a humoured and knowing tone. Having finished drawing a series of symbols in the circle, all connected by spokes which made the drawing almost resemble a cartwheel, he put the protection sigil to the side. He clasped his hands together, and leaned forwards. 'So you wouldn't say he was scared the other night?'

'No,' Toby repeated, seemingly frustrated with the grown-ups not quite getting it. 'We never said he was scared. We said he was a chicken.' Katie giggled, which seemed odd; neither she or Toby seemed too concerned by their father's mysterious disappearance, it only seemed to amuse them.

'And by chicken, you mean...?'

'Ba-kawk!' Toby squawked, holding up a crudely drawn image of a chicken for Sam to see.

In that moment, the occult detective's eyes widened. He felt pieces of fragmented ideas begin to fall into place, like a puzzle piecing itself together in front of his mind's eye. Simon's affectionate chicken, "Daddy's in the garden," the brood of chickens outside, the errant feather in the children's bedroom... He stopped himself from getting too carried away. It was an absurd theory, the evidence was merely circumstantial, no matter the correlation. *But still...* 'Do you remember what story he was telling you that night?'

Toby and Katie grinned, looked at each other, and began to chant in perfect unison, in what could be – depending on your personal opinions towards children – an adorable or creepy sing-song voice: 'I wish I was a chicken, I wouldn't have much to do; each day I'd lay an egg, and Sundays even two.' The children laughed, and Toby looked at Sam and Alice with a humoured smile. 'Daddy didn't even finish the rhyme before he clucked off.'

With a sinking sense of realisation, Sam knew that his absurd theory was true. Terrence Melville, landscape gardener, loving husband to Simon and father to Toby and Katie, considerate neighbour to the elderly Deirdre and Cedric Roberts, had not disappeared under mysterious circumstances. Nor had he fallen prey to a curse. Terrence Melville had, in fact, been transformed into a chicken.

'Daddy said he wished he was a chicken, and then he turned into one?' Alice asked the children. The idea was fermenting in her mind, too, but despite how the dots were all linked together, she wasn't quite willing to believe it; the day had already become quite absurd enough as it was. Toby and Katie nodded. 'Sam, are you thinking what I'm thinking?' She knew she didn't have to ask, the answer was almost certainly ludicrous enough to be true, but she thought maybe saying it out loud might help. 'Is Terry a literal chicken?' *Nope, did not make it any less weird.*

Leaning on the arm of the settee, Sam had torn a page from his notebook and was hastily scrawling something across it. 'One sec,' he said, the scratch of his pen on paper fast and erratic as he scribbled the last of the sentence, 'there we go.

So, in a word: yes. And I have an idea.' Sam held the piece of paper up for her to see. In the ambient light of the living room, she could see his scribbled handwriting spelling out a message: "I wish to be my human self again."

Simon leaned forward in his armchair, his elbows resting on his knees and his fists pressed against either side of his head. A look of quiet anger reflected in his face. 'You can not be serious?' he groaned, his eyes glaring at Sam and Alice from beneath his furiously furrowed brow. 'You have the audacity to come into my home, and then proceed to insult my intelligence by playing childish games. Games surrounding a very real and traumatic situation, I might add.' The glistening of tears welled in his eyes, although he still glowered at them just as fiercely. 'You're lucky I didn't call the police the moment I saw you on my doorstep.'

'Mister Melville,' Sam blustered, hoping to ease the situation before things took a turn for the worse, 'I assure you we mean no disrespect. We only want to do the best we can to help you and Terrence.'

'I understand how this must seem to you,' Alice said, her voice calm and pacifying, 'and honestly, if I was in your shoes, I'd feel the same way. But please believe me, we don't want to make things any more difficult than they already are for you.'

'You should've thought about that before you knocked on my door.'

'I know what you must think of us,' she

continued, 'but if we're correct, then this really might make everything right again. You just have to trust us.'

'That's a big *if*,' Simon groaned.

Refusing to be deterred by Simon's stand-offish demeanour, Alice smiled politely at him. 'Perhaps. And if we're wrong, if what we try doesn't work out, then we'll be out of your hair. We won't bother you again. We just ask for your patience for five more minutes.'

'Yeah, five minutes should be enough,' said Sam.

Simon's eyes softened. He was still angry with them both, and felt as if he was at his wits' end, but he considered Alice's suggestion. They were already back in his house, after all, what harm could five more minutes cause? Aside from taking advantage of his trauma and carrying on a – quite frankly disrespectful – practical joke for too long, they had not posed a threat to himself or his children. And when their little game didn't amount to anything, he could politely tell them to piss off and get the hell out of his house. Of course, he could do that right this moment, but something in the back of his mind was almost entertaining the idea that maybe they were right.

With a laboured and aggravated moan, he rubbed his temples and breathed, 'Go on, then.' He didn't look at them; he couldn't bear the self-congratulatory smug smirks he imagined they would have on their faces. 'But five minutes,' he stated, 'not a second longer.' He fixed them both with a stern stare, to make sure his point had landed, and much to his surprise his two interlopers appeared to be relieved.

'Thank you,' Sam said, bowing his head. 'Now that you've agreed to indulge us for another five minutes, I'm going to need some bird seed and access to your chicken coop.'

'Don't make me regret this,' Simon grunted.

Meanwhile, somewhere else in Highbury...

Several streets away, in a bedsit in a converted townhouse, an argument between two housemates was raging. Quite what had originally started the argument was anyone's guess, the quarrel long since having moved on from the original topic to a heated airing of grievances. Having to live together in the confines of a small North London flat-share rarely comes without its domestic disputes, and Aaron and Kaila had certainly found themselves embroiled in one.

'And then there's the dishes,' Kaila said, gesturing in the vague direction of the shared kitchen, her voice raised but not quite having broken the shout-barrier, 'when was the last time you even put on a pair of rubber gloves?'

'I did the washing up the other day!' Aaron argued back, his face turning a particularly visceral shade of red. 'What've the dishes even got to do with anything anyway?'

Kaila threw her hands up in exasperation. 'I wash up my stuff every day. And you know what else? This morning, and last night, there was already someone else's stuff in the sink that I had to get through first.'

'Well woop-dee-doo! Do you want a medal or something?' Aaron had transcended the realm of rational argument several minutes ago, and had instead devolved into defensive flippancy. Kaila stared at him in incredulous silence for a short while.

'No,' she eventually said, her tone lowering,

'it'd just be nice if you could acknowledge it. I'm not your maid, I'm your house-mate. We have to share a space, I'd appreciate it if we shared the responsibilities too.' She tried to smile weakly at him, feeling herself calming. They had been living in the same flat for almost a year now, and had been friends for several years before that; pissed off as she was, and whatever had led them to this point, it wasn't worth burning their bridges over. 'Sometimes I feel like you seem to think that your needs come first, before anyone else's.'

'I'm sorry,' Aaron said, addressing his feet as he gazed solemnly at the floor. Clutching his hand to his forehead, he took a couple of deep breaths. 'I'm just so busy with work, and working on my music any chance I get, I haven't got time to worry about housework.'

Kaila scoffed, but held her tongue from her immediate rebuttal. Instead, she too took a breath, and opted for something a little more diplomatic. 'Well, sorry to rain on your parade, but you're not the only person here who has other important things going on,' she said with a half-amused chuckle, 'we all have to balance our responsibilities.'

Before their discourse could continue, they were interrupted by a sudden noise. It sounded almost like trumpeting trombones, accompanied by the sharp staccato of snare drums, just below the window. Shooting confused glances at each other, Aaron and Kaila rushed to look out across the road.

Outside, a parade had come to a stop in the

middle of the street. Where it had come from, where it was going, and precisely why, remained unknown. The only thing which gave either of them any clue as to the parade's purpose was a large banner displaying, in big, bubbly letters, the words: "Aaron Has Important Things To Do."

The banner started to become flecked with droplets of water. Only a few at first, but progressively more and heavier drops of rain began to land on it. The letters began to run, with pale red streaks trickling down. The triumphant fanfare of the marching band fell silent, and they looked up to the sky in dismay as it began to rain on the parade.

'You are unbelievable,' Kaila grumbled, staring with disbelief at the marching band below them. She was incensed that he would go to such ludicrous lengths for, what? To appease his own ego? 'How- Why did you even arrange this shit?'

'Me?' This time, Aaron was the one to feel incensed at the accusation. 'I had nothing to do with this. You really think I'm that much of a narcissist? Why would I waste my time and money on a bloody parade?'

Kaila offered no answer. 'Wanker,' was all she said as she left the room, slamming the door behind her.

Watching through the rain-flecked window, Aaron stared at the strange and inexplicable sight. His mind boggled as he tried to process what, precisely, had just happened. The marchers were now hastily packing away their equipment, the parade now disrupted. Their formerly neat formation dispersed, as some took their leave and began to head off down the road, while others stood beneath the banner as a make-shift shelter.

'This is so weird...'

CHAPTER VII

It had started to rain since Sam and Alice had arrived at the Melvilles' place. It was, mercifully, not a particularly heavy rainfall, only a mere drizzle. Although, it had still clouded over an otherwise bright autumn's day, and it appeared that it was likely to get worse, too. A short distance away, the clouds seemed to be darker and heavier.

Urban foxes were somewhat of a nuisance in London's more residential regions – doubly so for anyone who kept chickens – and the coop in the Melvilles' back garden had been locked up for the night like a maximum security prison. Simon fiddled with the locks, flicked the latches aside, and opened up the doors to the hen house. Surprised by their impromptu night out, the hens ventured down the ramp and out into the garden, contentedly clucking about the lawn, fluttering their wings in the rain. They looked up with their beady eyes, blinking inquisitively at the three people gathered around their coop.

In his hands, Sam clutched a fistful of seeds and the piece of paper. Placing the paper carefully down upon the grass, trying his best to keep it dry, he knelt down by the side of it. 'Terry,' he addressed the chickens, 'Terrence Melville?' The birds tilted their heads at him quizzically, humming and clucking at the strange man. 'If you're here, Terry, I'm here to help you.' One of the chickens stepped forwards, tip-toeing closer to him, and he tried to figure out if it was the same bird he had met earlier that day. It was hard to tell.

Sam gestured towards the piece of paper on the ground, and rattled the seeds in his palm invitingly. 'Here you go, Terry,' he said, scattering them across the paper. He didn't know what he had expected, but the moment the seeds hit the ground the chickens all came charging towards him at once. The one which had stepped forwards, however, was ahead of the others, and darted towards the seeds at great haste. It pecked greedily at the piece of paper as the others began to swarm in, and Sam stepped back as the paper was engulfed in a sea of feathers.

'This was your supposedly bright idea?' Simon asked, raising a dubious eyebrow. 'Looks like it's working a treat.'

'It's not an exacting science,' he shot back, 'I have to try each possible avenue with this. Just give-'

Simon held up his hand, motioning for Sam to shut up. The occult detective obediently fell silent. 'No. I've indulged your foolishness as you asked. Now please, leave.'

'Wait!' Alice exclaimed, pushing herself between the two men and pointing at the chickens. 'Just look.'

In the middle of the thrum of hens, amidst the

fluttering blanket of orange and brown feathers and cacophony of clucks, something was happening. At the heart of the chicken cluster, one of them was beginning to shed its feathers.

'Oh good,' Simon grumbled, 'you've somehow managed to give one of them mange. Talk about adding insult to injury.'

The chicken in question did not have mange. Feathers fell from its body in plumes, its bare form began to change. The beak receded, its shape started to shift, the eyes changed from orange to blue. Featherless wings stretched out, strange appendages almost reminiscent of fingers began to protrude from their tips. The thing which had once looked like a chicken squawked a strange and terrible squawk, transitioning into the sound of a man's voice. Its body elongated, like clay being pulled and moulded into something new.

'You are kidding me...' Simon breathed in disbelief. His jaw hung open, and he felt his legs go numb. With the wretched crunching of bones, the fleshy sound of muscle and sinew being rewoven, and a confused, squawking shout, the changeling chicken was no more. In its place stood a man, about six-foot tall and with bright blue eyes, looking rather bewildered in his pyjamas and standing in amongst the chickens. 'Tear-bear?'

Terry's lips quivered and his eyes lit up in an expression of immense relief. Carefully stepping over the birds, his legs moving uncertainly now they were human legs again, he suddenly dashed towards his husband. Simon could barely contain his happiness, his smile wide and bright, and his eyes welled with tears. They wrapped their arms around each other tightly, holding one another close.

As they stepped back, slowly and reluctantly releasing each other from their embrace, Simon dabbed a tear from his eye. 'I can't believe it,' he whispered, his voice choking as he spoke, 'I just... I can't. I didn't know what had happened, but this...' He looked at Terry with a sorrowful expression. 'I thought you'd gone.'

'Oh you silly goose,' Terry said, rubbing his hand up and down Simon's arm reassuringly. He looked down at the chickens milling about his feet. He blinked confusedly, having not quite adapted to being so tall again. 'I wouldn't expect you'd even dream... This. But you couldn't really have believed I'd just "go" like that, could you?'

With a sniff and a solemn shake of his head, Simon stared down at his slippers. Although it still wasn't raining hard, they were starting to get a bit too damp for comfort. 'I don't know,' he sighed, 'you just disappeared. The kids said you were a chicken, but I didn't think they were being literal.' Something resembling wry amusement began to glimmer in his eyes and twitch upon the curve of his lips. 'And please don't call me a silly goose... I've seen what happens when you mention poultry.'

They laughed, though it barely disguised the confusing surge of emotions they were both feeling. Relief and joy that the spell had been broken, mournful for the heartache it had caused, sheer bewilderment that Terry had been a chicken for a few days. It was a lot to take in all at once.

With a pained smile, Simon turned to face Sam and Alice. 'I think you can understand my hesitance with everything going on,' he said, 'but I'm sorry I got so stand-offish with you. And thank you, for not letting it drop.'

'Of course,' Sam said. He wasn't entirely sure how to respond to Simon; the man had apologised, after all, but he also had an overwhelming urge to say, "Ha! Told you so." He considered it a sign of personal growth that he didn't.

'This one can get a bit feisty when it comes to protecting his family,' Terry said, patting his hand on Simon's chest.

'That's completely understandable,' Alice added, smiling at them. Having seen both Simon's worry for his husband and his defensiveness over his family, seeing he and his husband reunited warmed her heart. 'I'd have felt exactly the same. We did just burst into your lives with some outlandish stuff.'

'I'm very glad you did,' Simon beamed at her. He wrapped his arm around his husband's waist, and gave him a quick kiss. 'Let's get you inside,' he said, 'I think you deserve a better meal than just some old bird seed.'

'I noticed you've been stress-cooking these past couple of days,' Terry replied.

Rushing ahead of them both, Sam blocked their path and held up his hand. 'One more moment, sorry,' he said. 'Before you enjoy your evening, I have one thing I need you to do. Terry, now you're you again, could I ask you to command the djinn back into its vessel?'

'I'm sorry, what?'

'Just a quick little "I, Terrence Melville, command thee, djinn, to return to the vessel from which you were released."'

Terry cast a questioning glance to Simon, who could only offer a confused shrug in response. 'All right, fine,' he mused, and repeated the words Sam had just spoken. It felt awkward and strange speaking them, and he wasn't sure what precisely was meant to happen next. Even if he'd had an inkling, nothing could have prepared him for the reality.

Ahead of them, standing in the doorway back into the house, stood the shape of a person. Or, at least, something vaguely resembling the shape of a person. It was hard to see exactly what it was, as the manifestation appeared more like a heat-haze than anything else. The light from the kitchen seemed to bend and warp through the person's haze, the image of the dining table and chairs distorted and wavy on the other side of the invisible body standing in their path.

'What the hell is that?' Simon breathed, as his mind tried to make sense of the blurring heat-haze.

'That,' Sam said, folding his arms with an air of self-satisfaction, 'is the djinn. The genie responsible for this.' He took a couple of steps forwards, a stern expression written across his brow, fixing his stare roughly where he would expect the thing to have eyes. 'Now, djinn, you have been commanded to return to the vessel you are bound to. It's about time you popped along, don't you think?'

'No,' came the singular and defiant reply. Its voice was deep and resonant, echoing all around them, seemingly emanating from nowhere. And, with that response, the heat-haze began to dissipate. The intangible blur of the being's astral form vanished amidst a flurry of wisping, waving air.

Sam stood wide-eyed with disbelief, his gaze lingering on the spot where the djinn had almost manifest. 'That bastard,' he exclaimed, and turned to face the others. 'Well then, that didn't go quite to plan.'

'What was meant to happen?' Terry asked.

'It was meant to return to the vase it was released from.'

'And didn't it?' Simon followed. 'It did just disappear, how do you know it didn't vanish away to this vase?' He blinked repeatedly, looking to Terry with a curious expression. 'This is weird.'

'Didn't you hear the git?' Sam said, wildly gesticulating his arm in the vague vicinity where the heat-haze had appeared. 'It had the nerve to say "no," when it should be bound to obey your command.' Pacing agitatedly back and forth on the patio, while the rain gradually continued to soak through Terry's pyjamas, Sam tried to formulate a new plan. If the djinn was able to refuse Terry's command, he thought, then it must not see Terry as its master either. Despite fulfilling his wish to be human again. 'But how?'

'How what?' Alice asked.

'I'm just thinking out loud,' he said. 'How could the djinn be bound to enact Terry's wish, but refuse to obey his command to return to the vase?'

'Could we be dealing with yet another person who came into contact with it?' she pondered. 'I guess it ignored me because it was still technically bound to Terry too. It could be the same thing.'

Sam hummed contemplatively. 'Not impossible,' he said, considering the possibility. 'At this point, I'm worried it may already have gone rogue, though. Maybe it's been left unchecked for too long, with no one ordering it back into its vessel until today...'

'I'm sorry,' Terry said, 'I didn't know... Until I was already a chicken, but even then I was more confused than anything.'

'Of course you didn't know. Why would you have any reason to?' Sam meant it in a way to assuage any guilt Terry might have felt, but unfortunately – while he was in "thinking-out-loud" mode and not considering his tone – it sounded almost accusatory. 'No one knew what they were dealing with, so no one was able to enforce it. The spirit's contract has unwittingly been broken by its unknowing masters. Now, as it's already disobeying orders, if we don't act to contain it quickly, things could get really out of control. It's likely already spreading its influence through the local community.'

'So, what can we do?' Simon asked. He was still

trying to get his head around the situation, and a part of him still wasn't quite willing to believe it. If he hadn't have witnessed a chicken transforming into his husband, he'd have thought it was all bollocks. 'And do we really have to be out in the rain for this?'

'Fine,' Sam obliged, directing everyone towards the doorway while he continued. 'Normally, we'd just invoke the djinn's contract and it'd be bound to obey. But there's no one master for it anymore, so it's not that easy. We could try a summoning spell to recapture it and bind it again, but it's going to be difficult wrestling it away from its newfound freedom.'

Stepping over the threshold and out of the rain, standing in the dry and homely kitchen-diner, Alice had an idea. 'You say there's no *one* master,' she said, 'but there have been a few. Deirdre, Terry, Timmy, me... And, aside from me and Terry, I don't think anyone else would have tried to bind it again. What if we all invoked this "contract" you keep mentioning? At the same time?'

'Wait, Deirdre? Deirdre Roberts?' Terry seemed shocked, although the dawning realisation gradually came upon him. 'Oh. *That* vase...' he mused. 'She did say she felt there was something wrong with it.'

'Yes, *that* vase,' Sam said wearily. 'But actually, now you've said that, Alice, that's an intriguing point.' He stopped pacing about the kitchen, instead standing like a pensive statue, resting his chin in his hand thoughtfully. 'It might be a bit of a stretch, but if the djinn had been accidentally invoked by multiple people without being dismissed between each one, it stands to reason that no singular person could order it to return...' With a sudden burst of excitement, Sam wheeled around. 'Terry, I know you've only just transformed back from being a chicken, and I already said it was just one more favour, but I have another favour to ask. You too, Simon.'

The two men breathed something which almost sounded like a reluctant sigh. 'All right,' Simon said, 'what do you need from us?'

'Now that you can see I'm not talking complete bollocks, please indulge me for just an hour longer. We might just be able to put an end to this, but it's going to involve all of us. Alice, if you've got Deirdre's number on you, give her a call and ask her to meet us at the shop. We're going to need to get Judith and Timmy to join us there too.' He pointed towards the two men. 'Simon, Terry, bring your children as well.'

'Why? What are we going to do?' Terry asked, tilting his head at Sam with an expression of bird-like inquisitivity. He still seemed somewhat dazed and confused by all of this.

'We're going to catch ourselves a genie.'

CHAPTER VIII

Trapped, alone, and angry. That was all the djinn had known for almost a century and a half, although it felt like an eternity longer. Freedom, to roam as one pleases, to not be beholden to the commands of other – and lesser – beings, seemed all but a distant memory. Even his name was a half-forgotten fragment of a life that once was, known only as "the djinn" to the humans who had held him captive in this vase for so long.

His sentence had started sometime in the latter years of the nineteenth century, during the second Anglo-Afghan war, when a British officer with an inclination towards the occult had summoned him to a temple on the outskirts of Kandahar.

It had come some weeks after the British had suffered a disastrous defeat at Maiwand. Their forces were routed, retreating east to regroup at a more defensible position: the citadel of Kandahar. Not long after the straggling regiments had arrived at the citadel did they find themselves under siege by the forces of Ayub Khan. It was hard to say how long they had endured the battle, but the infantry were exhausted, morale was low, and the hope of survival – let alone victory – was dwindling. They expected a relief column from Kabul would arrive to reinforce them soon, but many were not sure they could hold out long enough.

After many a sleepless night, and too many friends lost to the field of battle, Lieutenant Hughes was at his wits' end. With each passing day he felt as if he was living on borrowed time, and with each brother-in-arms lost he was increasingly sure he didn't have much of it left. In the small hours of the morning, when the guns and cannons were silent, and only a few sentries remained awake to watch the perimeter, Hughes crept out of his bunk. He had heard legends of the spirits which drift upon the desert's night air, of their powers and how – with the right conditions – one might harness their magick. He sneaked out to a temple, just south-east of the city, and set about beginning his ceremony. A ceremony to call upon the djinn.

He sprinkled salt across the ground, forming the circle in which he was to perform his ritual, and sat upon the dusty floor of the temple. To the northern edge of the circle he placed the cleaned bone of a sheep's shoulder, and to the south he laid a square of red silk. He positioned flour and oil to the east, and to the west he scattered dust from the temple's door and shavings of aloeswood (acquired from a soldier in the Indian regiment). Upon the square of silk, he placed a vase – cast of iron, with ornate detailing in gold – reciting an incantation as he did so. A binding spell. Holding his arms aloft, he spoke into the space above the circle and its contents, calling upon the spirits, summoning an intelligence to aid him in his time of need.

And he waited.

While he waited, Hughes carefully etched a symbol into the cap of the vase. Should the spirits deign to answer his call, he would surely need means to seal them.

After an hour or two, when the sky began to lighten and the dawn threatened to break, the djinn answered the officer's call. He stepped through the veil between the aether and the earthly, crossing the threshold to the material plane and into the ritual circle. Revealing himself to Lieutenant Hughes, the djinn proposed the man with a deal; should he find the officer's cause worthy, the djinn would bestow upon him three wishes.

Hughes beseeched the spirit. He asked for the being's aid in battle, that he be safe from bullet and shrapnel, gun and sword. He prayed for the swift arrival of the relief column, and that with their reinforcements the battle would prove to be a victory for the British Empire. All they desired was peace, he said. And the djinn had listened, indifferent to the petty squabbles of human affairs, and asked why he should help.

It was then that Lieutenant Hughes – true to the British Empire's colonial reputation – sprung his trap. He revealed the binding spell which now tied the djinn to the vase, weakened by the iron and unable to escape the circle of salt. The spirit was shackled, its essence anchored to the terrestrial realm. Compelled by the magick which now ensnared him, Hughes explained, the djinn would be forced to obey his commands, obligated to carry out his three requests until the spirit's duties were fulfilled, and would be ordered back into captivity.

The djinn, unable to simply refuse these terms and depart, bowed his head in fealty and submission to the man who had ensnared him. Though he was forced to obey against his will, a resentment and loathing burned deep in his heart.

With the terms of the magickal contract now ratified, and the djinn having invoked his powers to Lieutenant Hughes's will, he was commanded back into the vase. Hughes then placed the cap – adorned with the symbol of the nine-pointed star – upon the vase, twisting it thrice, to ensure his captive genie would never escape its bonds for as long as the seal remained. Save only for when the djinn was summoned to enact the will of whomsoever possessed its vessel, to whom the djinn would be in servitude until their three wishes had been fulfilled, and it was sealed away once more.

As the sun began to crest over the horizon, Lieutenant Hughes made his way from the temple and back towards his regiment.

The Battle of Kandahar was to be the last conflict of the second Anglo-Afghan war. The relief column had arrived the following morning, bringing with it supplies and troops, as well as a renewed sense of hope. The next day, shortly after nine o'clock in the morning, the battle began in earnest, and had been declared a victory by lunchtime. It was a decisive victory for the British and Indian forces; Ayub Khan's defeat brought an end to the rebellion, and to the war. The djinn had fulfilled Lieutenant Hughes's wishes. Not that the officer had lived to witness it.

True to his word, the djinn had protected Hughes through the battle. The Lieutenant had cheated death at numerous turns, narrowly avoiding being struck by gunfire and stray shrapnel. What Hughes had not been expecting, however, was to be trampled by one of the horses that had broken loose during a lull in the fighting. It was a terrible shame, the djinn had thought, that Lieutenant Hughes hadn't had the forethought to wish for aid *outside* of the battle, too.

Following his death, Hughes's personal effects were packaged up and shipped back to England. Among them, an iron vase with gold details, firmly sealed with a cap. The djinn still trapped inside.

Although the man who had summoned, trapped, and commanded the djinn was now dead, the djinn was still bound by the magick he had weaved. He remained inside his iron prison, far removed from the old world, disconnected from the aethereal plane, unable to escape his cell. Time passed by slowly, and the djinn was cursed with the awareness of each passing second, though he soon lost count.

Probably around a decade or so later, the djinn felt the fresh air of freedom once more. A scholar who had been in search of items of a reportedly magickal nature had acquired the vase. Having studied the symbols Lieutenant Hughes had adorned the ornament with, he sought to unlock the potential of whatever enchanted essence was contained within. With three twists of the seal, the djinn saw the world beyond the vase again, and found himself in servitude of a new master.

Walter, as he soon learned was the scholar's name, was much more sparing in his use of the djinn's power. At first, it was the simple wish of being well-regarded in his field of study. Obligingly, the djinn presented him with the opportunity to take his career in academia further, affording him the platform to hold lectures on the arcane and its influences on civilisations through history. Amidst his successes, Walter felt no need to call on the djinn, though he kept the vase upon the mantel in his study.

It was another year before Walter made his second wish. He yearned for companionship, and though he had met with many a fascinating colleague in his field, he had yet to meet one he held close to his heart. Walter asked the djinn to bring him a wife. A few days later, after holding a seminar on the mythological roots of the Christian faith, Sophia entered his life. They enjoyed each other's company, shared many a night discussing history and mythology (among other, less academic, activities), and soon they were wed.

Again, the djinn found himself abandoned, existing in a prison which seemed to be little more than a talking point at parties. Meanwhile, Walter and Sophia enjoyed a happy marriage to one another, too wrapped up in their own bliss to consider the being who had brought them together.

Another three years passed, but as time wore on, so too did the magick. Their love began to sour. Sophia tired of her obligations as a housewife, while Walter became more absorbed with his career, which put a strain on their relationship with one another. One can not expect the magick to remain unless those involved are willing to continue working on it, which is true of love as much as it is life.

However, Walter still had one wish remaining, and he considered a solution to their problems. Were they wealthy, then Sophia's duties would be taken care of while she enjoyed the life of a lady, and Walter would work as and when it pleased him rather than out of necessity. He approached the djinn again, and wished for enough success and wealth that both he and Sophia would live in the lap of luxury, and have no need or want for anything. Although he had proven to be less duplicitous than Hughes, the djinn felt as if Walter saw him as nothing more than a wish-dispensing machine. Nonetheless, he was bound to fulfil this third and final wish.

Walter and Sophia found themselves moving to a manor house in Sussex, replete with staff to take care of their every need, and enough money to their names that they may live comfortably for two lifetimes. Once again, the djinn had made their dreams a reality; all the while, he remained trapped within his infernal iron prison. He grew jealous, and hateful, knowing they were living their lives to the fullest, care-free and at liberty to do as they pleased. Unlike him. Yet all because of him. Thus the djinn considered it only fair that it wasn't long before the Inland Revenue came knocking to investigate the sudden, inexplicable and undeclared wealth that Walter and Sophia had come into.

The manor was repossessed, their finances stripped from them, and Walter and Sophia found themselves destitute and dishonoured. Again, the djinn thought, it was their own fault for not specifying *how* they would come into such wealth.

The vase went up for auction, along with the rest of Walter and Sophia's estate, and was passed between a number of people over the following years. All of whom thought it to be merely an old ornament; none of whom bothered to unscrew the cap which kept the djinn locked inside. That was until the early nineteen-twenties, when the vase came into the ownership of a woman by the name of Stephanie. She inherited it from her father, who had also thought it was simply an old ornament.

It lived on a bookshelf in the living room for a short while until, one night, Stephanie decided to unscrew the cap. She had little to no idea of what power the vase contained, she simply felt compelled out of an inescapable curiosity to try and open it. It was a little stiff at first, not having been opened for many years, but eventually she twisted the cap free. Along with the djinn.

The sight of the apparition before her, manifesting first as a haze before taking the form of a man, caused her to shriek a most blood-curdling cry. Hearing the very obvious terror in his wife's voice, Stephanie's husband came rushing to her aide as fast as he could. The moment he lay eyes on the ghostly form drifting out of his late father-in-law's vase, he promptly fainted.

While Stephanie continued to shout for the ghost to go away and wrestled against her shaking hands to secure the cap back on again, she failed to notice that the paraffin lamp her unconscious husband had been carrying had rolled out of his hand. The fuel leaked across the floor, and flames began to lap at the curtains. For once, the djinn couldn't take credit for the calamity that had befallen the humans who had unwittingly released him (infernos often fell more within the purview of those spirits of fire, the ifrit), but he wasn't exactly upset for them either.

Thankfully – although much to the djinn's disappointment – Stephanie was able to seal the vase once more, and the fire brigade responded swiftly to the burgeoning blaze. Neither she or her husband were harmed, and their home only suffered some minor damage. Nevertheless, once they had recollected themselves after the abrupt chaos, they resolved to throw the haunted vase out. Which they did. Very quickly.

The vase was saved from heading to a landfill by a neighbour, who spotted the ornament waiting for the rubbish collection. It lived in his home for a few years, before being donated to charity. It passed between several people again, between friends and family, down through generations, decades passing, before being lost and forgotten in an attic somewhere in North London. All the while the djinn remained trapped inside his material prison, bound by metal and magick, growing more resentful and jealous with each passing moment. Envious and spiteful of the humans, who blithely went about their mundane and mediocre lives, while he remained confined within this minute prison. A pathetic existence for a powerful being.

Time passes by in a curious fashion when you're imprisoned inside a vase. Doubly so when you're a centuries-old elemental spirit from a dimension beyond the terrestrial plane. It was hard to differentiate one moment to the next, knowing nothing but the inside of the sealed vessel, and it felt as if it had been merely minutes while weeks had gone by, yet also as if eternity had passed in a single second.

In reality, it had in fact been nearly a century since the djinn had last been released from the vase. In that time, the ornament had found its way to an antique shop in Islington, where it had recently been purchased by one Deirdre Roberts. Little did she know she was about to find herself not only becoming the unwitting master to a djinn, but also his liberator.

CHAPTER IX

It had been so long since the vase had last been opened that the cap had rusted shut, becoming stubborn and unyielding to a simple twist-and-pull. However, Deirdre Roberts was similarly stubborn and unyielding. She had been determined to remove the cap and, with a sufficient amount of effort, she had managed to open it.

After a century of imprisonment, the djinn was once again taunted with the world beyond the vase, but still bereft of his freedom. No sooner had he felt the air and caught a glimmer of sunlight was he pressed into servitude yet again.

This time, he decided, he was not going to dignify another human with a formal greeting. They were beneath him, undeserving of his presence. All they ever did was use and abuse his powers anyway. No one had ever stipulated that he need manifest before them, after all; only that he fulfil their wishes. So he didn't bother shifting from his non-corporeal state. He could still obey their commands, albeit reluctantly, even as a zephyr.

What surprised him was the mundanity of

what his new master wished for. Almost as soon as he felt the bonds tie to Deirdre's commands, he heard her utter her first wish: for her husband to be quiet.

Normally, whether he had been invoked from the vase or summoned through a ritual in the old country centuries ago, people often wished for something greater. They would wish for things which would put them ahead of their competition, or for favours which would grant them wealth and success with far greater ease. Very rarely did they simply want the silence of a partner. It was unusual, but easy enough to accomplish.

With the grace of a summer's breeze, the djinn glided towards Cedric, reached into his open mouth, and stole his voice.

Perhaps being trapped in the vase for a century had lowered his expectations of people, but rather than being ordered into fulfilling another wish or compelled back into his cell, Deirdre asked nothing of the djinn. She neither wished for anything else, or replaced the seal on the vessel. Instead, she placed some magnolia trimmings into the vase, along with a little water. The djinn drifted, incorporeally, uncertainly, without direction. He would have relished this unexpected freedom, were it not for the fact that the magick kept him bound to the vase and his new – and seemingly unaware – master.

Perhaps, he considered, this woman was ignorant of what she held in her possession, much as Stephanie had been almost a hundred years before her. For a brief moment, he considered letting her know, but decided against it; he may not be wholly free, but he would be damned before he let another human do as they pleased while he languished in endless servitude. So he watched, and observed them go about their lives.

There was something almost comical about how Deirdre grew progressively more agitated at Cedric's silence. She had her wish granted, after all. Most people were grateful with getting what they wanted, even if only for a short while. Instead, this woman seemed irate at being gifted with her husband's silence, and as the days went by she only became more frustrated. Which made it all the more entertaining for the djinn. Though he could do little more than drift aimlessly around the Roberts' household, watching them was infinitely more amusing than being cooped up inside the vase again.

Eventually, Deirdre made her second wish. This time, she wished for Cedric to boil his head. She really seemed to have it in for her husband, the djinn thought. After stealing his voice, willing harm upon the man seemed unnecessarily cruel, especially from his own wife. She had said it with such flippancy, too, she clearly had no concern for the consequences. But the djinn was bound to obey, and carried out his orders. With an invisible hand, he pressed the poor old man's head into a pan of boiling water, amongst the potatoes.

Had he a voice with which to scream, Cedric's cries would have been deafening. All he could muster was a pathetic shriek from beneath the bubbling water. Which impressed the djinn; even with his voice magickally removed, Cedric still found the power to cry out in some way. This time, when Deirdre realised her wish had come true, she seemed more distraught than angry. For a woman who so frequently spoke of such cruelty befalling her husband, she certainly seemed concerned for his well-being.

Nothing more of interest happened over the next few days. Deirdre had Cedric rushed to the hospital, where she joined him and waited by his bedside, watching over him. The djinn watched over them too, albeit remotely, viewing them through the aether. There was little else for him to do while the Roberts were absent and the vase still in the living room. His freedom only extended so far from his prison and, although he was no longer trapped inside, he could not breach the four walls of the house. At least this new cell was somewhat roomier and more decorated, even if it wasn't to his taste.

There was, however, a television. An ingenious human invention, the likes of which the djinn had never seen before. It was not entirely dissimilar to remotely viewing things through the aether, although the television was bound by the physical laws of the material plane, reliant on crude electrical technologies and limited in its scope. It primarily presented pieces tailored to the humans' simple entertainment, often interspersed with a desperate bid to convince people to buy things, and updated them with an almost never-ending stream of news about the terrible things that terrible people had done. And sports, which were meant to be fun, but inspired a war-like fervour in a lot of people.

None of it inspired the djinn with a feeling of faith or love for humanity. If anything, it all made his loathing for them worsen. Especially daytime television.

It was oddly addicting, though.

A few days passed by. The djinn had learned much of the atrocities being committed in far-flung countries, and why committing similar atrocities in return was apparently perfectly acceptable. Whether something was good or bad seemed entirely dependent on who was doing it, according to the humans. He had watched an author hawking their new book to an overly-enthusiastic presenter on a morning talk-show, followed by a musical performance and an opinion piece on continental breakfasts. Then there was a seemingly endless stream of people arguing with each other, while a smug-looking presenter baited both parties against each other. After that, the djinn spent a couple of hours watching superhero cartoons as a palate cleanser.

Deirdre returned home that afternoon. She did not have Cedric with her, although according to a phone call she made, the djinn learned he was going to be fine. It was curious how this woman seemed more content with having her wishes undone than she was by having them invoked in the first place. If she hadn't wanted these things to happen, the djinn thought, she shouldn't have said any of them. It seemed like common sense, but if the television had taught the djinn anything, it was that humanity's baseline for sense and decency was lower than even he had thought.

It was late one evening when Deirdre ultimately made her third and final wish. She had grown lonely in her husband's absence, with nothing but her thoughts to keep her company through the quiet nights in this empty house, and she wished that she didn't feel so alone.

After the cruelty she had wished upon Cedric, and her apparent dismay when her wishes were manifest, the djinn wasn't convinced she deserved the comforting company he presumed she was asking for. After all, she didn't specify exactly *what kind* of company she wanted. And there was a certain pleasure to twisting a person's expectations for his own amusement.

So, in the dark of night, through the empty house while Deirdre was all alone, the djinn spoke to her. He still chose not to manifest himself before her, only to breathe his voice through the still air of the night. He told her she was not alone. As he watched the confusion on her face gradually turn into a creeping horror, he could almost feel the chill running down her spine.

When Deirdre began to sneak around the house in search of the voice, brandishing a torch as if it was a weapon, the djinn thought she could do with a little more "reassurance" that she wasn't on her own. In the dark corners of the house, he allowed himself to materialise – not fully, of course, that would give the game away – his zephyr-like essence shifting, taking form as a barely visible haze. Dancing about in the shadows on the edge of her torch-light, the djinn permitted Deirdre fleeting glimpses of something almost resembling his humanoid form, albeit intangible and on the very edge of perception.

After sunset each evening, he played this game with her. Speaking as a faint voice in the quiet of the night, casting haunting forms amidst the shadows, gently rattling objects – especially his own vase – to disturb the peace, opening and closing doors on the opposite side of the house. At least Deirdre never felt alone, although she was very much wishing she did.

Eventually, it seemed like enough was enough for the old woman. She rescued her magnolias from the vase, and threw the ornament out with the bins. This was another new experience for the djinn. Now that Deirdre had used her quota of wishes, she was no longer officially his master, but still she had not dismissed his service. Nor had she commanded him back inside the vase. Suddenly, he wasn't stuck within the walls of the house, but rather stuck outside and unable to enter. He still could not roam far, but it was a change of scenery nonetheless. No television, though.

It was then that he encountered Terrence Melville. The vase had remained outside, left untouched even when the bin collections had come and gone, and Deirdre desperately wanted to be rid of the accursed object. The djinn knew that feeling well. She had handed it to Terry, who promised her he would take it to the tip when he could, and left the vase sat on the wall outside.

Now, through this new contact with Terry, the djinn could roam both within his house and outside. Bit by bit, he could feel the invisible chains of the spell which bound him stretching. His potential for freedom growing.

Terry proved to be less fun than Deirdre at first. The man was annoyingly content with his life, and he seemed to not have much of a need or want for anything. The djinn wanted an excuse to sow some discord, to play around with this man's comfortable little life, but until Terry uttered a wish his hands were tied. He watched and waited, while the Melvilles went about their pleasant little existence as a happy family.

The children, Katie and Toby, made interesting wishes. Their minds took flight and explored fantasy realities, letting their imaginations roam freely. They wished for absurd and wonderful things; to be pirates sailing the seas; to captain starships which would take them to distant planets; for pet unicorns, or dragons, and to ride dinosaurs armed with lasers. The djinn was a little annoyed neither of them had picked up the vase. It would have been a worthy use of his powers, bringing such things to life.

Children, he thought, were not only more free with where their imaginations could take them, but also less prone to wishing for things to the detriment of others. They weren't immune to harbouring harmful thoughts – they were still only human, after all – but they had less of a capacity for callous cynicism. More of an innocence to their motivations. A child was more likely to make a wish for something fun, even if their wants were selfishly driven, than they were to will pain on another.

But the djinn couldn't bring any of these fantastical things to fruition. Instead, he was stuck waiting on the beck and call of tedious Terry. At least he could entertain himself with the cartoons the children were watching while he waited. Existing as a being of air and shadow, the djinn hovered unseen above the sofa, keeping amused with the shenanigans of the anthropomorphic animals on the television.

When Terry did make his first wish, the djinn was almost disappointed by how painfully plain it was. He wished his husband didn't have to work too much, and could spend the weekend with him and the kids. Not a command or a bid to attain power or riches, nothing adventurous or unusual, just a man simply wanting to have more quality time with his partner, and to have a nice family weekend together. It was a sweet sentiment, even if it was a little sad that it would take the supernatural powers of the djinn to keep Simon from having to work over a weekend. But it was simple enough, and the djinn saw to it with the blink of an eye.

There were documents with deadlines fast approaching, which suddenly had a week longer on them than Simon had originally thought. Files which needed reviewing and filing found themselves being very neatly, and most mysteriously, organised. Some paperwork plainly vanished into thin air. Much to Simon's confusion and delight, he had finished a lot of his work much sooner than he expected (and the rest of it could afford to wait another day or two), and he now unexpectedly had the weekend free. Free to enjoy time with his husband and children, and Terry's wish was fulfilled.

It was the second wish which brought the djinn much joy. Terry, Simon and the children had enjoyed a day out, picnicking in the nearby park, and the djinn had been able to follow them there. The limits of how far he could stray from the vase were apparently stretching further. That evening, when the children were settling into bed, and Simon was in the kitchen, Terry had gone upstairs to tell Toby and Katie a bedtime story. When he started to recite a little rhyme, he unwittingly fell into his second wish.

It was a silly verse about chickens. In some ways, the djinn resonated with the sentiment of the piece. It reflected on how chickens didn't have much to do, except for living their lives and laying eggs. He wouldn't have minded having such little responsibility. Although he sympathised with battery farmed hens, who – much like himself – were held captive and forced to produce to meet human demands. It seemed to be something humans were especially good at: subjugating things to satisfy their wants.

As Terry began to recite the opening line, the djinn saw this as his opportunity to have some fun. It may not have been a *real* wish, not in the strictest of terms, but a wish it still was. It technically fell within his remit.

With a sudden yelp, a squawk, and a flurry of feathers, Terrence Melville was transformed, to begin his new life as a bird. The ensuing chaos proved to be most entertaining. The children squealed with surprise and mirth at their dad's transformative performance, shrieking as they ducked for cover and ran about while their winged father flapped about the confines of their bedroom. After much poultry panic, Terry escaped the children's room, hopping down the steps on his chicken feet, and scurried towards the kitchen.

Inquisitively, he had poked his beak around the corner, staring with curious and beady eyes into the kitchen. Simon was hunched over, loading the plates and saucepans into the dishwasher. Terry clucked at his husband in the vain attempt at communicating with him. When he didn't seem to be listening, he rushed over and began to peck at Simon's trouser leg.

Now it was Simon's turn to be caught up in the commotion. Startled and confused to find that apparently not all of the chickens had been locked up for the night, he picked up a tea-towel and began to chase the bird around the room. All the while calling for Terry's help, although his shouts were not answered by anything more than confused clucking. He waved the tea-towel about as if he was a bull-fighter, clapped his hands to try and startle the chicken towards the back door, and eventually chased him outside. Unknowingly, he picked his husband up, holding his wings down tight, and locked him up in the chicken coop.

The antics caused by Terry's wish had been even more amusing than the djinn could've hoped. Simon was decidedly less than amused, though. When he went upstairs to see what Terry had been doing while he was busy trying to catch the chicken, and found his husband conspicuously missing, panic set in. It certainly didn't help when he asked the children where Terry had gone and they answered, quite honestly, that he was a chicken.

It wouldn't be fair to say that the djinn lacked empathy, but it also wouldn't be true to claim he felt any sympathy for Simon's distress. After so long trapped in the vase, and experiencing humans as cruel, conniving and controlling creatures, he had grown cold and uncaring to their suffering. None of them spared a thought for his suffering, after all, living their lives callously carefree while he wiled away in captivity. It seemed only right that he have his own back.

So when Simon spent the following day distraught, worried and confused over his husband's disappearance – ignorant to the fact that Terry was only a few yards away, pecking at seeds and nestling in a bed of soft wood shavings – the djinn laughed. It was almost ironic Simon should feel the absence of his love so profoundly, while Terry had often found himself missing spending time with his husband without the pressures of work on either of them. Now, neither of them could get on with much work, but nor could they relax into each other's company.

Perhaps this would teach them to embrace what they had, and not take even the simple pleasures in their lives for granted. The djinn knew all too well what it meant to have and to have lost. It frustrated him how frivolously humans lived life, not recognising its gifts or virtues until it was too late.

He did not have much time to enjoy watching Simon come to terms with this lesson, however, for another soon held the vase. A little boy by the name of Timothy Matthews had inquisitively picked up the vessel. Although his mother had made him put it back down almost instantly, the magick had already bound them.

A curious sensation came across the djinn. He was still bound to the vase, which sat on the Roberts' garden wall, while also being connected to Terry, who was now a chicken. He still had one more wish until the djinn's contractual obligations were fulfilled, even though in his present state he wasn't in a position to use it. And although Deirdre had used all three of her wishes, she still had not dismissed the djinn's service. Now, there was a third to whom the djinn was bound.

This had never happened before, and there wasn't a clause in the djinn's contract – as invoked by Lieutenant Hughes – which covered such an eventuality. The binding spell assumed the djinn would be in service to only one master at any given time, and that he would be confined again once his duties had been fulfilled. Now there were three concurrent "masters," none of whom were reinforcing the conditions of the spell which bound him. The magick was being stretched thin and, with it, so too were the metaphysical chains which shackled him.

Frustratingly, the aethereal plane remained out of reach. He was still bound to the earthly plane by the magick which tied him to the iron vase, and his obligations to fulfil three wishes to whomsoever commanded him were unchanged. Nonetheless, he was freer now than he had been in a hundred and fifty years, and he could feel his horizons broadening.

Not unlike the others of the djinn's most recent masters, Timmy was not yet aware of the power he could now wield. Although there was a decidedly more naive innocence about the way the boy thought. Much as the djinn had noticed with Toby and Katie, a child's wants were not yet corrupted by the machinations of an adult life. There was no underlying motive, no manipulation or abuse of power...

Timmy's first wish was for chocolate.

It wasn't quite the product of a child's immeasurable imagination as the djinn had been hoping for, but then Timmy didn't know what he was capable of. Yet. So the djinn decided to show him.

As he weaved the fabrics of reality together to conjure a hamper of chocolate delights, he allowed himself to manifest as well. There was a flash of ethereal bluish-white light as the djinn took form, stepping from his state as a being of air and crossing the threshold into corporeality.

He manifest as a man of indeterminate age – youthful in appearance, yet ancient in countenance – his almost ghost-like appearance standing before the boy, holding the hamper in front of him. He greeted Timmy with a friendly smile.

Timmy was, quite rightly, taken aback. He hadn't expected chocolate to materialise before him, least of all to be presented by a ghost who had suddenly appeared in his room. At first he was frightened, but the djinn kept a respectable distance from the boy, and attempted to put him at ease. He explained what he was – a djinn, a genie – and that he had the power to grant Timmy his truest wishes. One of which had been for chocolate, which he had already provided. As the djinn talked, Timmy listened on in wonderment, enrapturedly chewing on a bar of chocolate.

The promise of having his wishes come true was an understandably exciting one for Timmy. He was a wise boy, though, and knowing that already one of his wishes had been squandered on chocolate, he needed to put some thought into what his remaining two wishes would be. The djinn understood and, more than anything, appreciated the fact that the boy understood the true weight of this gift. Better the child take some time to think on what he wishes for, rather than blithely invoke them without a moment's consideration.

So the djinn departed, until Timmy was ready to make his next wish.

It was the following day that another curious

case occurred. The djinn's vase was being moved. He could sense it being pulled further away, and yet he was not being dragged along with it. It wasn't a short move either; not like it had been when it was moved from the mantelpiece to the garden wall. It was being taken considerably further than that. This wasn't an issue for him, though. It may still have been his prison, and his essence was inextricably bound to it, but it no longer ruled him; no longer confined him. If anything, this now allowed his reach to extend even further.

Especially when the vase changed hands. In her ignorance of the djinn's existence, rather than imprison him again (if she even could have done at this point), Deirdre instead got rid of the ornament by returning it to the shop. And so, another bond was made. This time, to a woman named Alice Carroll.

The djinn directed his consciousness down through Highbury, afloat on a breeze along the high street of Islington, and into the antique shop, where Alice was looking over the vase. She rubbed at the gilded details, and idly wished that she knew what precisely had got the old woman so flustered. Deirdre had not walked so far that it required any particular effort from the djinn, so with an invisible nudge back to the shop and a curious compulsion to tell of her experience, he invisibly directed Deirdre to answer Alice's wish.

He watched them for a while, the shop assistant and the old woman. There was something different about her. Not Deirdre; Alice.

There was an aura about her that set her apart from the others, something more "real," not quite as entrenched in the human conception of normality. Someone whose life was lived partly in the world around her, as well as in touch with the world beyond her, and within her.

It came as little surprise, then, that the djinn deduced that she could sense him. As Deirdre recounted her tale, Alice had given furtive glances towards the vase; he was certain she could feel his presence in that room. And, from the way she had listened to the old woman's story, she was likely going to believe her sixth sense.

Then there came another. A man, clad in a hat and jacket, who professed to be an occult detective. There was a similar essence about this Sam Hain, too, although the djinn got the sense that this man was more accustomed to – even more comfortable with – dealing with spirits than he was with people. For a moment, while Sam busied himself with waving a technological wand around the vase, the djinn thought he was about to be discovered.

Thankfully, despite his knowledge of the arcane arts, the occult detective was not quite as clever as he liked to pretend to be. And although Alice evidently had an intuitive instinct for the interdimensional, and had – to some extent or another – been aware of the djinn's presence, she hadn't been able to truly see or identify his aethereal form. Which he was grateful for; of all the people he had encountered, if anyone was able to imprison him in that accursed vase again, it would be these two.

The problem was, unaware as they were of his true nature, this wasn't the end of it. Sam and Alice were determined to look into matters further. They may have been labouring under the assumption everything was down to a curse, but they weren't stupid. It was only a matter of time before they would learn of the djinn, and sure enough they would lock him away inside his iron prison. He wasn't prepared to be bound within that infernal vase again, not now, not when he could sense his freedom was so close.

Were he not still bound by the wish-based rules placed upon him all those years ago, the djinn would have tried to stop them. Instead, all he could do was wait until a window of opportunity presented itself to him, and hope that they wouldn't trap him beforehand.

He watched as Sam and Alice spoke with Simon, asking questions about Terry's mysterious disappearance. It brought them a little too close for comfort, but the djinn assured himself it was fine. While the duo were still considering things through the lens of a suspected curse, they were too busy asking the wrong questions and looking for the wrong things.

The technological wand-like device had detected the djinn's presence, but neither of them had known what to make of this. Even Terry had tried to tell them what was going on, but – being a chicken – they couldn't understand his repeated clucking. They still seemed none the wiser about the djinn. If they remained ignorant of his presence for just a while longer, he thought, then he might just be able to throw off his shackles completely before they had a chance to stop him.

Satisfied with the would-be detectives wandering cluelessly around the Melvilles' house, the djinn became aware of another wish being made. Without a thought, he made it so. It was only when he noticed that the father and daughter, who were now having a heart-to-heart talk as a result of this wish, had not been in contact with the vase, that the djinn was truly aware of how lax his bonds had become. If he could now enact the wishes of people who had no ties to him or his vase, this opened up a new world of possibilities. He experimented with this, as the daughter wished her father could truly understand. So he did. The man felt the full brunt of her emotions in that instant, and began to weep.

This, the djinn thought, could be fun. Free to invoke the wishes of anyone he so chose...

It would have to wait, however, as Timmy had called upon his genie friend. The djinn's essence refocused and coalesced at the Matthews' residence, prepared to enact the boy's wish. And it was a good wish. Timmy asked to be able to fly, and so the djinn gave him the freedom he so craved; to be free of the inescapable pull of the terrestrial realm. Or, in Timmy's case, not limited by the force of gravity.

For the djinn, flying around in the material plane was akin to plodding through mud; it paled in comparison to the freedom and potential of the aethereal plane. But from a human's perspective, the joy they felt when no longer bound to the ground was the closest thing their squidgy biological bodies could achieve.

He kept a watchful eye as Timmy jumped on the trampoline, higher and higher, until eventually he simply didn't come back down. There was the added and quite unexpected pleasure of witnessing the boy's mother frantically running about on the ground, scared out of her wits that her child was stuck in the sky. There was something terribly pleasing about knowing how fearful humans were of the djinn's powers.

He didn't get to enjoy the entertainment for long, though. In fact, what came next almost threatened to ruin his fun altogether. Alice had made another wish, and this time it was for things to be a little bit easier. A hint, a clue, a sign pointing them towards the answer. The djinn's metaphysical heart sank. He had no desire to help them; if he did, it would bring them one step closer to trapping him. But he was duty-bound to fulfil the wish, and the causal threads which had brought them to this very moment had aligned just right.

At the same time as Timmy rose higher into the sky, and Judith became more desperate for help, the djinn prompted Sam and Alice's awareness of the flying boy.

As he had feared, it pointed them down the right path, and within moments the occult detective was reeling off his theories about dealing with djinn. Timmy, with all the naive innocence of a child, had told his mother about the genie, and she in turn had told the two who had come to help them. There came talk of trapping him in the vase again, and the djinn could sense this moment could lead to his undoing.

He couldn't let that happen. Not again. Not after so long. Not when he was so close.

That was when his window of opportunity opened up in front of him. It didn't come in the form of a wish – not precisely, anyway – but in the form of a casual saying. The word "wish" was in the sentence and, if he was being creative, the djinn considered this a loophole. As Alice told Sam to "knock himself out," the djinn gladly obliged.

Weaving his non-corporeal essence in just the right way, he seized Sam's body, forcing the man to grip the fencepost and slam his head into it. Knocking him out cold. With the occult detective out of the picture for the time being, and his companion uncertain as to what to do, the djinn had bought himself a little more time.

Something in the spell which bound him snapped. It was like an overstretched elastic band, pulled taut to the point it could no longer resist, and yielded. He remained tied to the vase, and still his freedom only seemed to extend as far as Highbury and Islington, but the rules which bound him to fulfil wishes had been broken. Presumably that loophole of wilfully misunderstanding a phrase had been the final straw.

Now, with the main threats to his freedom indisposed for the moment, he was going to make the most of it.

There was little the djinn could say he liked or respected about humanity, petulant and arrogant creatures that they were, but there was at least something he enjoyed about them. People had a terrible tendency to speak without thinking. Generally their mouths would flap and words would spill out in a manner that he thought seemed like a poor simulation of consciousness. Especially the politicians he had seen prattling on the news.

Often people would say things with little thought as to the real consequence of their idle babble. It was an infuriating habit, to be sure, but there was an upside. Now that the djinn had more freedom to act, he had a wealth of opportunity to twist their realities to fit their ill-chosen words.

Idioms were particularly fun for him. Little exaggerated metaphors which invoked peculiar imagery. They were enticing. Spoken more often than most wishes, too. With the contract of servitude all but discarded by his most recent string of "masters," he could exercise more of his trickster magick again. As he had done in the centuries before his imprisonment.

He manifest an eloquent executive equestrian near Highbury Fields, so that a woman may hear about her promotion straight from the horse's mouth. He made another woman see her boyfriend – and soon-to-be fiancé – as an adorable dog. He had conjured an entire marching band, only for it to rain on the parade.

Some poor, unsuspecting person was listening to their friend, and had claimed that they were all ears. They would have screamed, had the djinn not reshaped their body to be wholly composed of ears. When their companion yelped in shock and horror, though, they experienced an all-new definition for surround sound. When the friend had leapt back from the awful, auricle nightmare which sat across the table from him, he exclaimed "fuck me sideways!" in abject horror, and got more than he bargained for.

Elsewhere, someone was prefacing an argument by playing the devil's advocate, and instantly appeared in court. The defendant was a suspiciously horned man who not only looked guilty, but proud of the fact.

A troupe of actors performing at the Almeida theatre were rushed to hospital, all of them admitted with mysteriously broken legs. To add insult to injury, the director regretted stating that the production-halting incident was going to cost an arm and a leg.

To cut a long story short, it was a perfect storm.

Someone else wished they could have waffles for dinner and, sure enough, a plate of waffles materialised before them. For every interesting thing the djinn could conjure, there were a hundred plain and boring things.

However, the djinn's fun was put on hold. Something was different. He could no longer sense the connection to Timmy, or to Alice. He shifted his attention back to the road in Highbury where this had all started. He saw Timmy, no longer flying. His mother, no longer worried sick. Sam and Alice making their way back to Simon Melville's house. An aura of a different kind of magick surrounded them; judging by the radiance of her aura, it seemed that the Alice girl was responsible.

Whatever magick Alice had weaved, whatever concoction she had crafted, it had disconnected the djinn's bond from herself and Timmy. Robbing the boy of his third and final wish, and robbing the djinn of enacting it. The magick had severed their ties, undone his enchantments, and it seemed to be emitting a faint protective shield around them.

Protective, perhaps, but not impervious. Though he may not be linked to them anymore, and the effects of his magick on them had been rendered null, it might just be possible for a new wish – or even a saying – to break through. He proved himself right when Simon wished for Sam to leave him alone, and the djinn had been able to convince him to oblige. It didn't last long, though; Alice hadn't been affected by this wish, and had drawn Sam back. Evidently, as the caster of this particular magick, she was all but immune.

Evidently, the two detectives were devising a plan of action. A plan that would almost certainly mean the djinn would find himself confined within the vase, alone, powerless, crammed inside that dark and heavy prison.

It wasn't long until they had figured out what had happened to Terry, and found a way around the challenge of him being a chicken. Terry was the last of the people who the djinn was bound to by the old contractual obligations, and so enacted the man's – or rather, the chicken's – third and final wish when he pecked at the words on the paper. He reshaped the chicken back into its original form as Terrence Melville.

Then, once he had found his feet in human form again, Terry ordered the djinn back into the vase. There was a slight push and a pull, the last remnants of that original spell adrift in the Akasha, but the words held no power over the djinn. Not anymore. He could simply refuse to obey. He wove his essence before them, manifesting as a haze, to speak his defiance to them directly.

"No."

For well over a century, the djinn had not been able to say no. Lieutenant Hughes's magick had denied him that privilege. But now, he was free to act on his own will, beholden to no man. The fact that he could stand there and defy them in that moment was liberating. Exhilarating.

For as long as he could deny the orders of one of his former masters, he could get that one step closer to complete freedom.

CHAPTER X

Clouds gathered above Islington. Moments ago, it had still been a clear and bright autumn's eve, but now a blanket of slate-grey was ushering itself across the previously blue skies. What had started as a small, light drizzle in Highbury had grown, spreading out wider as the rain began to fall heavier. The smell of petrichor lingered in the air.

Hurrying along the high street, Sam and Alice rushed towards the antique shop, ducking their heads against the rain. It was almost refreshing at first, feeling the cool spatter of autumnal rain, but it was beginning to reach an unpleasant level. *When it rains, it pours.* Especially after a warm day, with the rainfall soaking into clothes which grew cloying, sticky and damp.

'You really think this will work?' Alice asked, casting a wary glance to the clouds above them.

Sam did not answer her immediately. He continued forwards, not breaking his stride as he marched purposefully towards the entrance to the narrow side-street. 'As far as I see it,' he said, rounding the corner, 'we have little choice in the matter.'

'That's not exactly an answer.'

They reached the antique shop just in time. The rain fell in fast and heavy droplets, and they sheltered in the narrow space of the store's awning. Fran had closed up the shop about half an hour before they arrived, which came as some relief to Alice. As much as she was now terribly aware that she hadn't returned to work before the end of the day, she would've dreaded having to explain what was going on to her still reasonably new employer. She fumbled in her jacket pocket, reaching for her copy of the key, and unlocked the door.

'Right, we've got about quarter of an hour before the others are supposed to get here,' Sam said, looking around the space as Alice set about turning on the lights. He'd asked the others to meet them there on the hour, hopefully giving him enough time to set the stage. 'Let's clear some space to set up this ritual.' Darting forwards, taking very little heed or care for the numerous and pricey antiques which adorned the place, he began to push furniture to the side.

Alice was scurrying backwards and forwards, trying to rescue as many of the smaller, more breakable, items she could foresee falling prey to Sam's reckless redecorating. Sam Hain's methods were consistent in one way, at least; one could always tell when he had been hard at work by the amount of broken objects, debris and chaos he often left in his wake.

'Please, be careful,' she implored, 'I'm already worried I wasn't back before Fran left. I don't want to add property damage on top of that.' She bundled together a collection of candlesticks in both hands, hurrying them to the safety of the desk at the back of the store.

Wooden furniture legs scraped and groaned across the floor, bundling up the Persian rugs which lined the routes for customers to follow. 'Don't tip that,' she called to him, moving the jewellery boxes which littered the top of a dresser. 'Don't move it yet, let me clear these,' she shouted, delicately picking up the items of a china tea set from a table, while Sam waited impatiently. 'Need a hand?' she asked, when she saw him struggling to move a bookcase, with all of the books still on it.

'Nope,' he grunted, 'I've got it.' With a few heaving groans, Sam was inching the bookcase across the floor. It was bulky and inexplicably heavy, and try as he might Sam hadn't been able to lift it. The best he could do was to move it a little bit at a time, dragging and pushing it inch by inch.

Eventually, when the space in the centre of the shop had been cleared, and all of the furniture had been shoved indelicately and haphazardly to the side, Sam stood triumphantly in the middle of the clearing. He seemed particularly pleased with himself, having brought this chaos upon an otherwise quaint antique shop. 'There,' he said with a sense of finality, 'now the real work begins.'

'So what do we do?' Alice asked, edging a glass cabinet a little further away from him. 'Or am I better off just making sure you don't wreak any more havoc?'

'The most important thing now is to cast the sigil. Our guests should be arriving soon, I'd like to have things as ready as possible.' He reached into his pocket, retrieving a piece of chalk, and knelt upon the ground. 'How hard can drawing a nine-pointed star be, anyway?' He set about drawing the symbol, scraping the chalk along the bare floorboards. 'Oh, if you happen to have any candles lying around, that would be excellent. One for each point, if possible, please. If not, we'll just have to improvise.'

While Sam was occupying himself with drawing the pattern on the floor, Alice began to search around in the back room. She hadn't seen any candles lying around before, but she suspected Fran would at least have a collection of tealights tucked away somewhere. She rifled through drawers and rummaged through cupboards, until eventually she found some. There were about five stick candles in a box, and three rather dusty tealights. *Bugger*, she thought as she hurried back into the room. 'I've only got eight.'

'That's fine,' Sam said, although it really didn't sound as if things were fine. His voice came from between gritted teeth, and his breath heaved with exasperation. 'How bloody hard does drawing a nine-pointed star have to be, anyway? I keep bollocksing the thing up.'

'Hang on,' she said, heading over to where she had left the collection of candlesticks and picking them up. Kneeling down on the floor next to him, she placed five of the candlesticks, and then the tealights, down in an almost circular shape. They were approximately evenly spaced apart, aside from a larger gap for the ninth – and still missing – candle. 'Now if you used each of these as a point, you can kind of zigzag from one side to the other.' As she spoke, Sam was following her instructions.

'That,' he said in a long, drawn out way, as he dragged the chalk along the floor from one point down to the opposite, then up again to the next one along in a clockwise pattern. He was having decidedly more luck drawing the pattern already. 'That might just work. When did you become an expert on geometry, anyway?'

'Former art student, remember?' she said with a wry smile. 'You get used to memorising quick and easy ways to draw certain shapes.'

From behind them, they heard the chiming of the bell as the door gingerly opened. They turned around and saw the familiar face of Deirdre Roberts. She was looking a little bedraggled, her blouse darkened in damp patches from the rain, and her hair had escaped its curls and started to frizz. She shook the water from her umbrella outside, and shut the door as she entered. 'Hello,' she said with a confused smile, 'what's all this?'

'Hey, Deirdre,' Alice said, standing to greet her. 'We've learned a lot more about your vase, and the genie it housed-'

'Genie?'

'Yes, genie. So, what we're planning to do is to – quite literally – put the genie back in the bottle, and we're going to need your help too.' She gave the old woman a kindly smile. 'So thank you for joining us.'

'Oh, that's all right, love,' Deirdre replied, 'just let me know what you need of me.' Alice took her umbrella, hanging it from the coat rack by the door, and directed her to one of the chairs which hadn't been pushed into the corner at an awkward angle. 'Anyway, better being in here than out there. It's raining cats and dogs at the minute.'

Deirdre really should have chosen her words more carefully. The consistent – and usually relaxing – sound of the pattering of rain on concrete and splashing of puddles was replaced by the wailing cacophony of cats meowing and dogs barking.

Yelps and mews echoed through the air as many small, furry animals plummeted from the sky. Along Islington High Street, pedestrians rushed to escape the sudden torrential downpour of poodles and Persian cats. They scurried hither and thither, fleeing to reach shelter and hide from whatever unnatural force was pelting them with a plague of pets. As they ran, people found themselves dodging and bounding over the particularly visceral and macabre puddles created from the downpour. Cats were fairly adept at landing on their feet; not all dogs had been quite so lucky.

A stream of shorthairs ran down the alleyway, flowing past the antique shop's window. Sam had stood up from drawing the sigil and was gazing out at the sight, his mouth agape. 'Deirdre,' he sighed, 'I mean this in the nicest way possible. Please, don't say anything.' Deirdre nodded, although it was hard to tell whether she had taken what he said seriously, or she was simply dumbfounded by the sight as well.

'What's going on?' Alice whispered, turning to Sam with a perplexed expression. 'That wasn't even a wish, was it? This doesn't make any sense.'

'It's worse than I thought,' he said, 'it's no longer just wish fulfilment; it's idiom invocation, a particularly ironic form of magickal manifestation. It's like when someone intentionally misunderstands what you're saying, or takes your words literally at face value, only it makes it real. And,' Sam continued, crouching down again, 'given our djinn's wilful misunderstanding of what people mean and ironic sense of humour, we need to rein it in before someone says something they'll really regret.'

Sam finished off the last of the star's nine points. He drew the binding circle around the pattern, curving the line from point to point as he went, and he sketched a few quick, rudimentary protection symbols around the outside of it. The sigil was complete. All that remained now was to add a final candle, and for the others to arrive to complete the ritual. Although quite how they were faring in this weird weather was anyone's guess. 'Alice, if we haven't got another candle for the final point, can you find a torch or lamp or something, please?'

Stepping over him and taking care not to accidentally smudge the chalk lines on the floor, Alice reached across to a wonky cabinet. 'Will this do?' she asked, holding up an art deco style table lamp.

'Perfect.' He gestured to the empty space in the circle of candles. 'Place the thing in the thing,' he said, informatively, 'and plug it in somewhere.'

Crawling along the perimeter of the wall of furniture, Alice tried to look for a plug socket. She knew there was one somewhere along the wall, but with everything now piled up in front of it it was hard to see. Weaving herself between table legs, she disappeared beneath the furniture. Thankfully, the lamp's cable was reasonably long.

The bell above the door chimed again as the others arrived. Judith and the Melvilles (which, in the author's opinion, sounds like a rather boring band name) had bumped into each other by the side-street, just as it had started to rain cats and dogs. They had clearly hurried to the shop as fast as they could, looking worn and worried, harrowed expressions behind their eyes. They had managed to keep their children reasonably sheltered from the unpleasant side of the sudden pet storm, mercifully avoiding the worst of it. The kids didn't seem too perturbed by the increasingly strange events, more enthralled with all of the fluffy animals now flooding the streets.

'What on earth is going on out there?' Simon exclaimed, making sure everyone was safely inside. He gently nudged a cat back out of the door with his foot, before closing it behind them. 'It's pandemonium.'

'Don't tempt it,' Sam warned, casting a wary eye towards the window. The last thing he wanted to deal with was anything from a John Milton epic poem. Thankfully, the world beyond the window still resembled a normal side-street in Islington (aside from the abnormal amount of cats and dogs), and not a sequence from *Paradise Lost*. 'I'm glad you're all here now. If you can just bear with us a few moments, we're nearly ready, and we can stop this rogue djinn before it goes too far.'

'You think cats and dogs dropping out of the sky isn't already too far?' Judith seemed incredulous at the idea.

'Much too far,' he said sombrely. 'Normally the impact of a supernatural event is either easily contained, or we've dealt with it before things have bled through too prominently in a public capacity. But this...' He trailed off, gazing out of the window and still glimpsing one or two pets falling to the ground. He pinched the bridge of his nose. 'This time, the cat is well and truly out of the bag.'

Judith hastily dropped her handbag. It squirmed and wiggled on the floor for a moment, before the fluffy head of a Maine Coon cat poked its head out from inside. It was hard to tell who was more surprised; the onlookers, or the cat who had found itself inexplicably materialising inside someone's handbag. With a graceful bound, the feline leapt from the bag and scurried towards the window, pawing at the glass. While the children fussed over the cat, who seemed more eager to get out than be cuddled, Terry opened the door. The cat jumped down from the window, slinked out of the door, and began to trot contentedly down the alleyway.

'See?' Sam said.

There came the sound of something scraping against the wall, followed by a click, and the lamp suddenly came to life. It bathed the room in its warm, orange glow. Alice's head poked out from underneath a table. 'Sam, we're about to summon and trap a genie. You can just make sure none of this ever happened with a single wish.'

'Maybe,' he said, 'we'll just have to bargain with it, find out what it's conditions are once we've bound it here.' Adjusting the candles to make sure each of them lined up perfectly with the points of the star, Sam stepped back and looked at his handicraft. Some of the lines were a little bit wonky in places, but that was to be expected. Beyond that, the sigil was near-on perfect. 'We're set. Thanks for the help, Alice.'

'Of course,' she said with a smile, 'any time.' Easing herself up and out from under the table, she dusted off her hands. 'Shall I start lighting the candles now?'

'Please. Let's create some calming mood lighting for our mystical guest.' He retrieved his lighter and tossed it over to her. 'I doubt he's going to be in a relaxed space once we draw him here.' Glancing over his shoulder, he looked towards the others; his magickal conduits to invoke the djinn.

Katie, Toby and Timmy had taken to fiddling with some of the antique ornaments and looking out of the window with mystified intrigue; a light rain of kittens and chihuahuas bounced off of the shop's awning, landing in the alley and scampering off. Simon was keeping an eye on the children, making sure they didn't break anything, gently taking the more fragile-looking objects from them while they kept themselves entertained. As utterly inexplicable as this all was, he was grateful that the viscera of the poodle puddles he had glimpsed earlier were nowhere in sight of the window.

Meanwhile, Terry was telling Judith and Deirdre about his time as a chicken, while they listened with concerned and confused expressions.

Sam turned his attention back to the circle, where Alice was crawling from candle to candle.

Beginning from the lamp, which she saw to be the topmost point of the sigil, Alice had been moving around the circle in a clockwise formation, lighting each candle as she went. A while back, when they hadn't been wrapped up in some supernatural situation, Sam had walked her through some of the basic steps of traditional ceremonial magic, and the words had stuck with her since. Clockwise for invoking the energies, anti-clockwise for dispelling them.

The star with rays of nine, Sam thought, *one for each of us around this sign*. Sometimes, these things often worked out even better than he had planned.

On top of a dresser, Sam had found a pair of old silk gloves – much more suited for a well-to-do lady attending the opera than for his occult practices, but they would do – and he now stretched them on over his hands. With great trepidation, he approached the desk where the vase was sat, still with its "Reserved: Do Not Touch" sign. He wasn't sure if the gloves would provide any meaningful protection, or whether Alice's spell would be enough on its own – especially now that the djinn had just invoked one of Sam's idioms – but he wasn't taking any chances. He reached out, carefully picking up the vase with both hands, and muttered something beneath his breath. Alice couldn't quite make out the words, but she was sure it was some kind of protection incantation.

He placed the vase delicately down on the floor, in the very middle of the formation where the lines converged and formed a nonagon. 'Right,' he said, pulling the gloves from his fingers and tossing them to the side, 'we should be ready.'

As he looked up to address the others, something caught Sam's eye. It was a collection of curious items on one of the shelves. Old, brass pieces of nautical paraphernalia and pocket watches, the kinds of accessories he imagined a character in a Jules Verne story would carry with them at all times. There was something peculiarly aesthetic about the antiquated devices. That being so, the sextants and compasses were of little interest to him in that moment; the thing which had caught his eye was a spherical object, composed of a series of interlocking rings surrounding a globe in the middle.

'An armillary sphere,' he said, as he leaned across and picked up the object, 'a three-dimensional astrolabe. Quite literally "the one who catches the heavenly bodies."' He held it for a moment, looking at it meaningfully.

'I love those things,' Alice said, standing by the

side of him, 'can't think of any reason I'd need to use one, but they look cool.'

'Well, now here's a use for one; as a tool for catching something not entirely earthly.' Gently, he began to fiddle with the mechanism. Twisting and turning the rings, slowly rotating them around the globe at their core. It was like watching someone try to work out a Rubik's Cube; only spherical, and without bright colours to show how wrong you are. He was rotating the sphere through the ecliptic plane, turning the signs of the zodiac about, and tinkering with the angle of the meridian. Judging by the expression on his face, he wasn't one hundred percent sure what the correct settings should be.

Eventually, with a decisive nod and a tilt of the meridian so that it rested at a sixty-five degree angle, Sam seemed like he was content. He traced the tip of the TechnoWand along the rim of the horizon disc, a soft hum and gentle glow resonating between the two devices. Taking care not to catch his trousers on fire as he stepped over the candles, he placed the sphere on one of the vertices of the star, the apex of the meridian pointing north, towards the vase.

'Okay,' he said, standing up and positioning himself by the art deco lamp on the floor, 'here we go. Everyone, if you please, take a place around the circle.' Sam gestured for them to join him, pointing them to the tips of each of the star's nine points. Once everyone was in position, he began to talk them through what they were about to do.

'You are all here because you have, in some way or another, been affected by the djinn and its powers. Whether you freed it from its vessel, unknowingly had command of it, or experienced its effects first-hand, you have had direct contact with the spirit. Unfortunately, as none of us knew what we were dealing with until a few hours ago, the djinn wasn't ordered back into its vessel between each "master," breaking the conditions which bind it. Instead, its contracts overlapped with all of you.' The assembled group watched and listened to Sam speak, nodding along politely, even if they weren't fully following the situation.

'Now the djinn is no longer under anyone's control and is running amok,' Sam continued, 'who better to rein it in than us?' He beamed at them. 'If we all summon it here, in unison, when it hears the order from its most recent masters at the same time, in the same place, with the same command, it will be forced to comply.' *I hope*, he thought.

'So what is it we'll be doing precisely?' Deirdre asked, raising her hand as if they were in a classroom.

'I've devised an incantation, all you need to do is repeat after-' Sam was interrupted by the sound of the bell above the door chiming again. He glanced around the circle, at everyone assembled. No one was missing and, as far as he knew, he wasn't expecting anyone else to join them. Turning his attention to the door, he saw a woman come rushing in. She was visibly agitated, her clothes damp and her raincoat flecked with droplets of water and the tell-tale red remnants of viscera.

She shuddered as she closed the door behind her. 'I didn't think you'd still be open,' she said, not yet having looked up at the environment inside the shop. She hadn't noticed the group gathered in a circle around an occult symbol. She pulled back the hood of her raincoat, shaking out her hair and running her fingers through it. 'You would not believe the weather we're having. I-' The woman trailed off the moment she glanced towards the others. Her eyes darted from the symbol on the floor, the burning candles, the nine people standing around it.

As if stepping in from it, quite literally, raining cats and dogs wasn't already disturbing enough, she found herself faced with an occult ritual. In a quaint antique shop, of all places.

'Oh for god's sake,' she exhaled, her voice trembling with worry and the unmistakable tone of someone who had quite frankly had enough of their day. 'It's Hell in a hand-basket today!' She spoke with a fearful frustration, although she said the words as if they were a merely inconsequential remark. If only her words had been as inconsequential as she thought.

A wicker picnic basket, trimmed with a red gingham cloth, materialised on the tabletop in front of her. The woman's eyes widened, simultaneously mystified and unnerved by yet another absurd occurrence. In some ways, it was a good thing she hadn't got the saying exactly right; things could've been considerably worse. She muttered something beneath her breath as she took a step forward, quizzically reaching out to the magically appearing basket.

'I bloody dare you!' Sam bellowed as he saw her approaching it. If there was one thing today had taught him, it was that nothing good could possibly come of this. 'Whatever you do, do not open that basket.' He broke from the circle and tried to rush to stop her, but with the ring of candles and the people gathered around the sigil, as well as antique furniture blocking his path, it was like running an obstacle course.

It was already too late, however. He couldn't have reached her any quicker than she could have lifted the lid of the picnic basket. Which she did.

The wails and screams of a thousand tormented souls filled the shop, echoing from the unfathomable and dimensionally quite impossible depths of the hand-basket. Infernal flames lashed up from the open lid, the inescapable smell of sulphur hung in the air. The woman stared into the whirling vortex of chaos and pain beneath the wicker lid. 'Oh no,' she breathed, and although she was terrified by the sight before her, she was also transfixed, unable to take her eyes away from it.

With the snapping sound of the lid slamming shut, she too snapped out of her trance. The flames were instantly suppressed and the terrible screams were all but silenced, only faint and muffled beneath the wicker and the gingham cloth. The smell of sulphur didn't dissipate quite as quickly, though. The woman looked up, her haunted eyes now meeting Sam's gaze. He stood over the basket, a hand firmly pressed against the lid.

'The next time someone says for you to not do something,' he intoned, like a particularly frustrated parent scolding a disobedient child, 'a word of advice: don't do it.'

He glowered at her, his eyes boring into hers, both out of frustration and in an effort to gauge how much she had seen. Had she looked upon the contents of the basket for too long, he thought, would've been to know madness. As far as he could tell, her sanity remained intact; shaken and disturbed, but intact. Beneath his hand, he could feel the basket forcefully quaking, and he found himself pressing down against the lid even harder, as something threatened to try and force its way out. 'What did you see in there?'

She was quite understandably afraid. Her skin had turned pallid and clammy, her eyes wide as if she had been woken with a jolt from a nightmare. 'I don't know,' she spoke in a hesitant manner, 'it was all... Impossible. Hellish.' She blinked rapidly, as if trying to dislodge the image from her eyes. Again, she took in the sight of the ritual, the candles in a circle around the strange and arcane symbol drawn on the floor. 'Just what is going on here? Is this all your doing? What weird, cultist shit are you people up to?'

Keeping a tight grip on the picnic basket's lid, which leapt up every now and again as whatever was inside struggled to escape, Sam breathed an exasperated sigh. 'Just get out,' he said. There was no polite cover story he could spin, no comfortable lie to mask what this woman had unfortunately already seen, all he could do was get her to leave before she got caught up in any more chaos. Or worse, cause any more of it. When the woman failed to leave after his first request, uncomfortably dithering on the spot, Sam tried shouting at her instead. 'Get out! Now!' A part of him felt guilty for losing his temper, and with a more cordial and gentle voice he added, 'please.'

The woman didn't need to be told a third time. She had leapt back in alarm, and with a curt and affronted remark she turned on her heels. Pulling her hood back up, she stepped out of the door, being sure to give it a disapproving slam behind her as she left.

Sam exhaled, which immediately turned into a grunt as the basket tried to escape his grasp once more. Both hands now gripped the lid, holding it tightly shut. Judging by the strange, jerking sensation, he could only assume something was throwing itself at the inside of the lid. 'Alice, a hand please,' he called over to her, and smiled to the others still standing, somewhat bewildered, around the sigil. 'Don't worry, this is perfectly under control.'

He was lying, of course, but he wouldn't admit it.

A lick of flame lapped out from a narrow gap as the lid was forced up once more. A faint shriek and something deeper, more guttural, primal and monstrous growled. Sam pressed his weight down upon the basket, hoping he could contain whatever was trying to get out until he had a solution. Problematic as it was, he was grateful her misquoted idiom had only resulted in this. A relatively small gateway to Hell, handily localised inside a picnic basket, was just about manageable. But only just.

Alice hurried over to Sam's side, placing her hands on the lid also, gripping it tight. She could feel the thumping vibrations of whatever was on the other side reverberating through the wicker strands. Muffled sounds of agonised screams emanated from somewhere deep inside. She wished this was the only strange and unsettling thing she'd experienced all day, but there were a number of contenders for that particular spot.

'Right, what do we do?' she asked.

'I don't bloody know,' Sam hissed, 'I'd prepared for a djinn, not this!' With Alice firmly holding onto the lid, he began to slowly remove his hands from the basket. If she could keep a hold of it for a while longer, he might be able to figure out a more permanent solution. He hoped.

Tracing the tip of the TechnoWand around the rim of the basket, Sam began to utter an incantation. Or at least, that seemed to be what he was doing. His lips moved rapidly, though Alice could hear no words being spoken. He kept his eyes focused on the wand as he continued to run it along the groove where the lid met the body, almost as if he was welding the basket shut. The device emitted an unpleasantly discordant tone as he worked.

'There,' he said, tapping the wand against the lid of the basket. Everything about his demeanour was as if he'd just sorted it all out, but his voice suggested otherwise. 'That should hold for a little while, at least.' He slipped the TechnoWand back into his pocket and ran his fingers through his hair as he thought. 'Problem is, it's not literally Hell in a hand-basket. It's a portal to its own pocket dimension, a subdomain of Hell, contained within an otherwise perfectly normal picnic basket. I can't seal off the gateway, not properly, but I can at least magickally lock the basket. For a few minutes, anyway.'

Carefully lifting her hands from the basket, Alice took a slow step back. The wicker creaked, the basket jostled about, but nothing came bursting through the lid. Sam's sealing spell had evidently worked. 'Okay, so we're not in any immediate danger?' she asked, and Sam made a facial expression which suggested that maybe danger was a little more immediate than any of them would have liked. 'Oh,' she said.

Sam lowered his voice, leaning across the basket as he spoke. 'It won't hold for long, but I thought it'd buy us at least a little time to come up with a plan,' he hushed. This was something he hadn't anticipated having to deal with; sealing off a pocket dimension is no mean feat. It would take time to figure out the best way of shutting down this particular portal, but time was not something they had a lot of. The demonic grunting from inside the picnic basket was a vivid reminder of that. 'It's time to get your thinking cap on, Alice!' he said, plastering on a forced smile.

With that, a baseball cap with a light bulb embroidered on the front of it materialised above

Alice. A second after it had popped into existence, gravity took hold and the hat dropped down, landing perfectly onto her head, the cap slightly slanting over her eyes. She grabbed it, pulling it from her head and giving it a look of indignation. 'Careful,' she said, almost lecturing, 'everything we say has very real consequences.' She tossed the cap to the side, but as she watched it spinning away and landing with a thud on an old armchair, a thought occurred to her. It might have been a shot in the dark, but it would be worth a try.

'I have an idea,' Alice began, 'words have power, after all, especially now apparently. You manifested a thinking cap with a simple turn of phrase.' The embroidered light bulb on the cap seemed to flicker with an ethereal light, as if in recognition of its mention. Or maybe it was just to show that it was working. 'So I'm going to try something, and if that doesn't work, we'll just keep trying until Hell freezes over!'

A cold, crisp, cracking sound came from somewhere inside the picnic basket. The force from the other side had stopped, and the basket was decidedly cooler to the touch. Tentatively, Alice lifted the lid, and cautiously peered inside.

No flames lashed up from the open lid this time; instead, there was a sudden gust of chilled, icy air. The screams of the damned had fallen silent, replaced by the bony clacking sound of a million teeth chattering. From somewhere deep within the abyss within the picnic basket, a voice cried out, 'Beelzebub's sake, someone put the heating on!'

For a brief moment, Alice caught a glimpse of what was inside. The nightmarish hellscape beneath the wicker lid spanned a long way down, an incomprehensibly deep pit. Rock bridges criss-crossed the chasm, some natural and some built by unknown forces. Unearthly, cyclopean structures and twisting fortresses jutted out from rock faces, on platforms and built into the side of the walls. All of them built at incomprehensible angles, with distorted dimensions. And all of them now gleaming, coated in glistening ice crystals, everything still and frozen in place.

Beyond it all lay the pit, impossibly deep and dark. Abyssal, unspeakable, and ravenous. A gaping maw ripped in reality, endless depths harbouring things yet unknown. At once impossible to comprehend, yet captivating. Enticing one to look closer, to learn of that which lies ever deeper.

The lid of the picnic basket snapped shut again, and Alice snapped back to reality. 'That might just be a pocket dimension,' she said, 'but it's more than enough for my liking.'

The antique shop may have been a state, with the furniture shoved unceremoniously to the sides and ornaments positioned precariously, but it was reassuring. It conformed to the usual understanding of perception and dimensional space, at least. Not like the picnic basket based plane. 'It looks like it worked, though,' she added proudly, 'it's like the Snow Queen's palace in there now.'

'Well, that's one thing we can cross off our list,'

Sam said, his face the image of relief, 'one hellscape frozen in place.' His eyes sparkled as he gave Alice a prideful smile. 'And good plan with combatting an idiom with another idiom. Very quick thinking.' Turning back to the others, who had broken their formation to sit down and lean against furniture while they waited, he clapped his hands together.

'Right then. Let's try this again, shall we?'

CHAPTER XI

Candlelight flickered about the feet of the nine as they stood assembled around the sigil.

His legs astride the art deco lamp on the floor, Sam Hain stood with his arms held out before him, his palms facing the ceiling. He cast his eyes around the circle, from one person to the next. They stood looking at him with an equal mix of attentiveness and curiosity. The children were starting to fidget, though; despite the excitement of what had been going on, there was something fundamentally boring about standing in a circle in the middle of an antique shop.

Confident that everyone was now ready, he cleared his throat to begin. 'Okay, now repeat after me.' Sam started to recite the incantation, line by line. The eight others around the circle repeated them back to him, as if he was leading in a prayer. In a way, he supposed, maybe he was. He might have been tempted to have everyone recite it in a round, but now was hardly the time.

Their voices resonated around the room as they intoned the words, speaking in unison, their voices calling forth the djinn.

'Great spirit of air and of shadow;
Being born from the smokeless flame.
We, who stand upon the nine-rayed star,
Command thee here, from whence thee came.
Djinn, we summon thee.'

Outside, the wind and the recent influx of dogs began to howl. Clouds swirled overhead, thicker and darker, looming ominously over Islington. Trees were blown back and forth, as if caught in a hurricane. A gale rushed through the streets, lifting leaves high into the air and stripping the newspaper stands outside of the underground station.

Then, in an instant, everything fell still. The streets were now mostly abandoned, pedestrians having fled and taken cover, but any who had remained outside would have noticed the change. It was as if the atmosphere had suddenly been siphoned elsewhere. The rain stopped falling, as did the cats and the dogs, and the wind ceased blustering.

Inside the antique shop, however, was a different story. The air around the circle whirled. Clothes and hair billowed and swept as the gust of wind whipped around everyone gathered there. Even the shadows in the corners of the store seemed to be blown about. In the heart of it, above the sigil, something began to form. A twisting heat-haze rippled above them, swirling around and down towards the vase in a vortex. The flames of the candles were blown horizontal, but they did not extinguish.

A current of electricity ran along the binding

circle on the floor, energy crackling and sparking. Light pulsed between the points of the star, coursing through the lines like blood through veins. Converging on the spherical astrolabe. They could almost feel the thrum of the pulse humming through the floor.

It was as if the astrolabe was a conduit for the energy. It seemed to be drawing the energy into its core, where it condensed and manifested as a ball of milky-white light. The orb of energy glowed in the heart of the mechanism, shining through the brass rings which encircled it. These seemed to be working to focus the energy, and through the meridian's apex it projected the light towards the vase.

The vase began to quake. Its iron body rattled against the bare floorboards, and it started to glow with an ethereal, bright bluish light. Everybody stepped back from the circle. The children hid behind their parents, clutching at their clothes nervously. As the haze continued to spin around itself, it started to grow more visible. More tangible. A shape resembling the outline of a person formed in the air, beginning to emit a brilliant white light, faintly glowing with the same aura as the vase.

With one twisting, whirlwind motion, the djinn manifest. He appeared in the form of a man, albeit considerably taller than most. His face was strong, a sharp jawline and defined cheekbones, although that may have just been the aura highlighting the outlines of his features. It was hard to tell; much of the djinn's appearance was either ethereal and only faintly visible, or wreathed in ghostly light. The vibrant energy rippled across his form, light dancing like unearthly flames, wisping and shimmering in a haze, around the shape of his astral body.

Where one might have expected to see legs, however, there were none. Instead, the djinn's body tapered into strands of ethereal energy, thin wisps of a faint blue force trailing down towards the lid of the vase. He looked upon those assembled around him, a dour expression written across the ghostly features of his face.

'Who dares summon me here?' the djinn spoke, his voice deep and commanding, laced with anger.

'We did,' Sam said, taking a step forward and standing toe-to-toe with the boundary of the binding circle. 'Hello.'

The others kept their distance, their mouths and eyes wide, caught in an emotion somewhere between awe and fear of the sight which had manifested before them. All except Alice, who was a little more used to seeing this sort of thing. Not that it diminished the experience.

'You know not of the powers with which you meddle.'

Sam smiled and nodded with feigned patience. 'Uh-huh, perhaps,' he said, 'but I don't think you quite give us credit for what we do know.' He gestured towards the others, who seemed less than keen on being introduced to the ethereal being. 'You already know everyone, right? Your recent – and quite accidental, I might add – masters. Or, perhaps I should say victims.'

He fixed his gaze on the two orbs which burned like icy fire in the djinn's head, presumably the spirit's eyes. If he was going to get the djinn under control, Sam knew he had to show it who was in charge here. Namely, himself. 'I figured, seeing as each of them failed to dismiss you from service, until no one individual could claim to truly command you... Well, what better than to get everyone together? You might be able to refuse one, but I doubted you could resist them all at once. I'm glad to see I was right.'

'I was finally free!' the djinn roared. 'I was released from that accursed prison. My chains were slack and loose. I could be free of having to bow to the petty needs of humans.' If the being were not composed of aetheric air and elemental energy, it would have spat. 'Now, in your hubris, you dare try to trap me once more?' In a whirlwind of fury, the djinn flew at Sam.

The occult detective stood his ground, his feet on the line of the binding circle, as the spirit lunged for him.

There was a strange, static buzzing sound as the djinn came to an abrupt stop mere inches from Sam's face. His nose crumpled as if pressed against a pane of glass, and veins of electric energy rippled out around where he had impacted the magickal barrier. Despite himself, Sam had flinched as the being got a little too close for comfort, although he knew the djinn could do him no harm. The circle around the sigil, and the magickal symbols he had scribed around the edge, should see to that.

The spirit eyed the empty space between himself and Sam with a mix of confusion and frustration. He lurched forwards again, only to be met by that same crackling barrier. He pummelled at the invisible shield with his fists, sending flashes of lightning-like energy rippling through the air, but to no avail. From what Alice could tell, watching as the energy sparked in protest to the djinn's attempts, everything within the circle was contained beneath an energetic dome.

His essence still trailing back to the vase as if it were a tether, the djinn turned about and flew at the others gathered nearby. They instinctively leapt back, not only terrified of the unearthly apparition, but also of what he might do if he were to break free. Watching their faces fraught with fear was almost amusing to the djinn; were it not for the fact that he was once again being contained against his will. It came as a relief to all assembled that the djinn yet again found himself running into the barrier.

Swimming around and around like a goldfish in a bowl, the djinn yelled in anguish. 'What have you done?' The white light which glowed about his aethereal form flared, burning so dazzlingly bright that it stung the eyes of anyone who looked directly at it.

'Taken the necessary precautions,' Sam replied, casually gesturing down at the chalk lines drawn upon the floor, waving his hands at the candles which surrounded them, and pointing to the astrolabe at the base of the vase. 'You've been causing more than a little bit of chaos, and I couldn't allow you to continue. Not when your powers can have disastrous consequences.'

'Then you seek to bind me once more, and subject me to your will?' The djinn made another futile effort to breach the boundary.

'Not exactly. I want to make a deal.'

'A deal, you say?' the djinn spoke, tilting his head towards Sam, a curious expression on his face. His burning white aura still shone bright, but it softened somewhat. 'Why should I believe your proposal? You would not be the first to try to deceive me with an alleged agreement.'

'No,' Sam said, 'no deception. I mean what I say. I'm willing to come to an agreement if you are. If not,' he gestured to the vase, 'you go back in there. But I get the impression that's not something you're particularly keen on, and I'd rather you didn't force my hand.'

'Then why do you bind me so?' the djinn asked. The last time a sorcerer had bound the djinn against his will, it had led to over a century of servitude. He wasn't likely to trust another human so soon. 'Why do you summon me, only to trap me?'

'Because you're causing suffering,' Sam retorted, almost reprimanding the being, 'and I can't let that continue. I won't just stand idly by while you torment and torture people. But that's why I want to make a deal. I ask something of you, and you get something in return. That's got to be better than fulfilling the wishes of any old idiot who picks up that vase, right?'

'Hey!' Deirdre and Terry exclaimed in unison. Sam waved his hand to shush them. Although he cared about their well-being, he wasn't going to concern himself with their sensibilities. He had only needed them there to help facilitate the ritual and summon the djinn; if not, he would have preferred they'd stayed safely at home.

The djinn contemplated this for a moment. He hummed over the idea, narrowing his eyes at the sorcerer who had trapped him, and glanced towards the others. They who had unwittingly invoked his powers, and who had accidentally given him a taste of freedom once more. 'And what is it you believe you can offer me?' he asked.

'That's up to you,' Sam replied. He paced about the edge of the circle. 'I could get you a latte from down the road, buy you a fashionable hat...' The djinn began to smoulder again. 'Or, perhaps, I could set you free from the ties that bind you?'

'I was already free!' the djinn protested. 'Until you summoned me here.'

'We both know that's a lie,' Sam said. 'Something keeps you connected to this vase. And clearly you're still bonded to those who have invoked you in some way, too, otherwise you wouldn't be stuck here talking with us now. For as long as that's true, I don't believe you can truly be free. Why else would you still be here, causing chaos?'

'To toy with you humans,' the djinn answered bluntly, not wanting to weaken his image in front of the lesser beings. He knew the occult detective was right, though; for as long as he was still bound to the vase, he would not be able to fully return to the aether. He could never truly be free.

'You've been doing more than toying with us,' Alice said, standing alongside Sam at the edge of the binding circle, 'you've inflicted pain and misfortune on these people, and who knows how many others by now.'

'Trapped for over a century, used as little more than a slave to some self-absorbed simpleton's whims...' The others would have objected at the djinn's insinuation, had they not been afraid of agitating him further. Not after everything he had already done. 'One requires some entertainment as recompense for all those years of imprisonment.'

Alice stared the djinn in the smouldering orbs of his eyes. As he snapped his attention to her, it felt as if they were burning into her. 'That's not the point though, is it?' she said, overcoming the djinn's attempt at intimidation. 'I can understand getting bitter and twisted, being trapped for that long. And for the way others have treated you. But these are innocent people you've hurt. They didn't trap you in the vase, and they wouldn't have meant you any harm.'

'Wouldn't they?' he bit back. 'Or would they have used me for their own gain as everyone else has, free to live their lives as they please while I languish in captivity?' He stopped himself short. Putting his wounded pride aside, he knew the promise of his liberty was far more important than justifying his actions to beings who couldn't possibly comprehend. He turned his attention towards Sam again. 'But that is the past. For now,

I shall hear out your request. State what it is you propose, and perhaps we can broker this deal of yours. Provided you agree to set me free.'

'Agreed,' Sam said, clasping his hands together. 'I'd like to propose that I undo your bindings to the vase, properly release you from whatever magick keeps you tied to it. You would be truly free.'

'Are you sure this is a good idea?' Alice asked, leaning in to whisper in Sam's ear. Although judging by the djinn's demeanour, it wouldn't have mattered if she'd whispered it or shouted it. Being a non-corporeal entity which exists beyond the physical limitations of human anatomy evidently meant its hearing worked in a different fashion.

'Trust me,' he hushed back with a look he hoped was reassuring, 'it'll work.' He hoped it would work. Turning back towards the djinn, he continued, 'And, in exchange, I only have two conditions. Firstly, that you will undo everything that-'

'I can not do that,' the djinn replied factually, with a stone-faced expression.

'Well, if you're already unwilling to make this deal, then it looks like you're going to be spending a long time in that cosy little iron vase of yours.'

'I do not mean that I will not,' the djinn hastened to correct himself. His demeanour changed. With the prospect of freedom hanging in the balance, he wasn't willing to risk it. He knew he would have to appeal to the humans, much as he was loath to. It was that, or face indefinite imprisonment again. 'I mean that I can not. I am a djinn, I have many powers. But I can not turn to the past and correct prior wrongs. What has been done can not be undone.'

'Oh, right, I see what you mean,' Sam said, 'sorry.' He looked sheepishly up at the apparition of a man, wreathed in the white and ethereal glow and floating in the air above the vase. 'It's my first time dealing with a djinn, you see. I'm not a hundred percent on the rules.'

'That is acceptable,' he acknowledged, bowing his head in understanding. 'Though it takes a powerful sorcerer to summon and bind my kind, it takes a wise one to know how to deal with a djinn.'

Alice let out a snorting, squeaking sound as she tried to suppress a giggle. Something about the manner in which the djinn had given Sam a back-handed compliment had struck her as funny. She cleared her throat, hoping it masked her amusement. 'If we can't undo what's happened,' she said, 'could we perhaps wish to minimise the impact of any of this? Maybe even make it so that it's almost as if none of it ever happened?'

'That would be a possibility, indeed,' the djinn intoned. 'And then you will release me of my bonds?'

'If you accept our agreement,' Sam said, 'yes. First we use your wish-fulfilling powers to set things right, and fix what you've done. Once that's done, then you will be free to go. As long as you agree to not meddle in human affairs, or toy with unsuspecting people, and return to your own dimension. No games or unexpected twists.'

The djinn considered this proposition intently,

seemingly having to deliberate over the idea of not toying with anyone once he was released. It was not an easy choice; it was cathartic playing with the expectations of humans, upending their otherwise uneventful little lives and watching as they struggled against anything remotely beyond their mundane existences. But, he considered, if the choice was to leave the humans well enough alone, or face being imprisoned indefinitely in that vase again, that was something he would just have to accept. 'Very well,' he spoke, 'I accept your terms for this agreement.'

'Excellent,' Sam said, punctuating his exclamation with a singular clap. 'And good thinking, Alice,' he added. 'Now, give me a moment...'

'I have no moments to give; there is only now.' The djinn opened his arms wide, holding his palms out to them, demonstrating that indeed he did not have any moments to grant them.

'I honestly don't know if you're intentionally obtuse or really can't tell the difference,' Sam said, 'but that was a figure of speech, not something I wanted you to manifest. I need a moment while I think.'

'We could start by changing people's memories of events, if that's allowed?' Alice suggested. 'If you can't undo things that have happened, we could make people forget the weirdest bits, at least. Replace their memories with something a little more... Normal?'

'That can be done,' the djinn obliged, 'though many will still recall some moments as though they were a distant dream.'

That was the thing about memories: the more unusual they were, the more memorable they had a habit of being; but also, the less believable they tended to be. The more obscure memories – such as those involving cats and dogs raining from the sky, or talking horses – could simply be rewritten as dreams or flights of fancy, instead of being the recollection of real events. Manifestations which were adjacent to accepted normality, however, would be a little more tricky to tweak. They were almost too believable, too grounded in reality, for them to be dismissed as a product of the imagination. However, this also meant they were probably things which were of such little consequence in the grand scheme that it mattered not; they would easily be forgotten in time.

'What about us?' Simon asked, stepping forward from the huddle of bystanders. 'Do we get a say in this? Because as much as I would hate to relive these past few days,' he took Terry's hand in his, 'I don't want to forget, either.'

'Me neither,' Deirdre chimed in. 'It was horrible, but lord knows I'll be appreciating Ced's company a lot more when he's home. Even if he can be a boring old sod sometimes.'

'And I was flying,' Timmy added, 'it was so cool. I don't want to forget.'

'Lucky,' Toby uttered, looking over to Timmy with awe and envy.

The djinn looked to the others. They'd experienced everything they had because of their own human hubris. As far as he was concerned, he could hardly be blamed for the realities they had brought on themselves; he merely enabled them. They had behaved as if they were entitled to whatever they pleased, to say and do as they pleased, while taking what they did have for granted. They had been careless with their words, no thought to the consequences of their actions, wrapped up only in their own self-centred concerns. Not that any of them were aware of this, of course; they were only human.

He had opened their eyes to this, however, shown them the damage their words could cause, made them confront themselves when the comfort of normality was stripped from them. He had taken a particular glee in manifesting the more absurd things, watching the creatures squirm as their reality became warped. Then he looked to the children, who not only had accepted the magick he had manifest without worry, but had wished with the purest of intents.

'Those who have been a part of this ritual,' the djinn spoke, 'will retain their memories of what has passed. What they choose to do with this knowledge is their choice.'

'In which case,' Sam said, 'I wish it so. May other people's memories of the strange and magickal events invoked by the djinn be changed, replaced with belief in thoughts of a more normal day.'

'As you wish,' the djinn said with a courteous bow. He spun about in the air, clicked his fingers, and a glowing ripple across his face twisted into something resembling a smile. 'Thus it is done.

Henceforth, those who have witnessed these events this day shall not recall them, save only as the faint echoes of dreams upon the midnight air. Instead, they are safe in the comforting illusion of a mundane Monday, as your kind would find more conceivable.'

'Excellent,' Sam said, resting his hand on Alice's shoulder. 'Further to that, I would wish that any evidence of today's events disappear, or be corrected to be in line with people's new memories.' He knew all too well that anything remotely outlandish would almost certainly have been captured digitally by at least one person's phone, or on CCTV. He wondered how many people would've stopped to take a video of it raining cats and dogs.

'No photos or videos of anything abnormal you've caused, no poodle puddles on the street, anything that can be erased without undoing the past,' he continued, 'and where things can't be undone, adjust them to fit the way people now remember today.' Sam didn't want to be caught out by a loophole in the metaphysical system, and hoped that this would cover all eventualities.

The djinn snapped his fingers once more. As he did so, the picnic basket – which contained more devils than it did devilled eggs – on the other side of the shop faded from reality. Outside, the cats and dogs which had fallen from the sky (as well as the macabre marks left by those that hadn't survived) were no longer bound by the laws of gravity. They began to float up into the sky, back to the place from which the djinn had created them.

'And thus it is done. Evidence of what has transpired this day, be it the physical manifestations I have conjured or the records people may have kept, are no more. That which can not be undone will appear to have rational explanations.'

'That's perfect, thank you,' Sam said, bowing his head respectfully. 'And now that things have been put to rights, I release you.'

Touching the TechnoWand to the binding circle, the device began to hum. The air around the circle rippled, the crackling dome-like shape of the magickal barrier which encased the sigil and the djinn retracted down and into the floor. The djinn watched the magick dissolve, almost in disbelief. Aiming the wand towards the vase, Sam began to utter another spell. 'Binding spells be undone, this djinn's obligations now are none. Beholden to no mortal's mastery, from your prison I set you free.'

A burst of energy crackled from the crystalline tip of the TechnoWand, arcing through the space between it and the vase. Electricity wreathed the iron vessel, fizzling across its surface. There was a popping sound as the energy propelled the lid from the top of the vase, sending it clattering to the floor. At the same time, the glow surrounding the vase faded, and the faint wisps which tied the essence of the djinn to the vessel broke free. The last fragments of the magick dispersed, disappearing like dust scattered in the wind.

'There,' Sam said, twirling the wand between

his fingers and sliding it into his jacket pocket, 'you are officially released. You can return to your own realm.'

'You would simply free me, you truly mean no deception?' The djinn asked, and Sam nodded. He looked down to the vase; once his preternatural prison, now nothing more than an empty metal vessel. The djinn's face was the image of wonderment. The wisping essence of his being no longer bound to the accursed thing. Though his form still glowed with that ghostly white, ethereal essence, the blue hues of energy which tied him to the vase had faded.

The djinn stretched and took a deep breath, as if this was the first time he had truly been able to breathe. He grinned with insuppressible happiness. The ghostly light which shimmered and gleamed across his astral body shone even brighter, though decidedly less fiercely, than it had before.

Testing the extent of his alleged freedom, the djinn started to fly. He began by simply drifting this way and that, but soon he flew from the confines of the sigil beneath him and soared around the room. The people who had once commanded him ducked and flinched as he flew overhead. He circled around the shop, flying above their heads as he embraced the sudden release. No shackles, no servitude, and no subterfuge.

Returning to the spot in the middle of the sigil, he hovered before Sam and Alice. 'Thank you,' the djinn spoke with a respectful bow, although he seemed almost confused. 'Though many have used me for their own selfish gain, you trapped me here yet have shown me kindness. Why?'

'Well, you were captured, taken from your own realm and forced into servitude, no one deserves that. A deal's a deal,' Sam replied. 'Although maybe I'm being a little selfish, too. I don't want to keep dealing with the havoc you've caused. Whatever helps you bugger off and leave people alone, the better.'

The djinn gave him an amused smile. 'Still, you could have imprisoned me again. Yet you did not. I can not express my gratitude. True to my word, I will not meddle in your mortal affairs, and shall depart to the aethereal plane. But first, you still have one wish remaining.'

'Oh no,' Sam exclaimed, emphatically waving his hands, 'no I don't.'

'It is the way. You successfully summoned me, bound me with your magick, you are entitled to three wishes. Though you have released me of my burdens and I am no longer obligated to serve, allow me to grant you this benefaction for your benevolence.'

Sam laughed, a nervous and dubious laugh. 'I've seen how you interpret and twist these things,' he said, 'I'm not going to take that risk. Anyone else?' He glanced around the room to the others, those who'd had their idle thoughts and sentences manifest in cruel and literal ways. 'Any takers?'

Everyone immediately shuffled backwards. They glanced at the djinn, instantly averting their gaze so as to not make eye contact with the being. They had endured enough already. The children clamoured for the opportunity to make a wish themselves, but their parents protectively held them back, and tried to cover the kids' excited shouts with their own protestations. There was a murmuration of "no," "that's quite all right," and "oh dear god, no, please, not again" as their answers filled the air. The djinn seemed almost disappointed that none of them were willing to accept one more wish from him; although, he could hardly blame them, after all they had been subjected to.

'You know,' Alice spoke up through the crowd's mumblings of distrust, 'aside from making Sam knock himself out, I don't think you twisted my wishes. As far as I can tell, anyway.'

'I followed your wishes to the letter. As I did for every one of you,' he replied. 'Though you can not deny that was amusing. I have learned much from your cartoons; slapstick is the pinnacle of comedy.'

Alice chose to ignore that last part. 'If you fulfil requests to the letter, and I leave you no room for misinterpretation or cruel irony, then I might have one for you.' The djinn tilted his head towards her in eager anticipation. 'I wish to know something secret, something true, something I don't know.'

Drifting through the air, slowly closing the gap between them, the djinn hovered next to Alice. He leaned in, his words caressing her ear like a warm summer's breeze. 'He is not what he seems,' he whispered, 'that you will know soon enough.'

The djinn pulled back, floating proudly in the middle of the room. 'And so,' he declared, 'I shall bid you all farewell, and express my gratitude for freeing me. But first, a parting gift.' Clapping his hands together twice, reality suddenly lurched. The room twisted around itself, blurring as it seemed to tumble through dimensions not quite of its own. Shapes warping, melding, dispersing like oil on the surface of water. As the world began to settle, the vague forms of furniture becoming solid once more, everybody looked around themselves.

The shop was back to normal. Furniture was no longer shoved against the walls, instead each thing took its rightful place throughout the store. Rugs were rolled back out along the floor, all traces of the chalk sigil wiped clean. A collection of candles – half-melted, but extinguished – lay on the counter next to the till. Everything was as it had been when the day began.

The djinn was gone, too. He had vanished into thin air, somewhere in amongst the dimensional turbulence, presumably having crossed the threshold from the material plane to return to his own realm. Everything fell still and quiet and, for the first time since each of them had invoked the djinn, everyone felt as if a dark cloud had parted.

'What did he say to you?' Sam asked, sidling over towards Alice. She looked at him curiously, as if she was trying hard to focus on him, almost scanning him. 'You okay?'

Alice blinked at him. 'Yeah,' she breathed,

'yeah, I'm all right. Just... My brain's still trying to process everything. He said...' She paused, looking at Sam standing beside her, smiling kindly. It wasn't a lie; she had barely had a moment to consider what the djinn had said to her before the world suddenly spun around them. Was it an insight? A premonition? A warning? She hadn't settled on an answer yet. All she knew was that the words niggled at the back of her mind. Uncertain. Wary. *He is not what he seems.* 'He said... He said that we would know soon enough.'

'Ooh,' Sam said, his smile turning into a grin, 'cryptic and ominous.'

'Yeah,' she said, offering him a vague smile in return, 'I know.' Clearing her throat, she turned her attention to the space around them. It was hard to imagine the state the shop had been in mere moments before. Everything was where it belonged, nothing broken or missing, all was as it should be. Fran would have no idea of what had taken place there that evening. 'At least we don't have to worry about tidying this place up now.'

'Well, that was... Something,' Terry said, wiping his hand across his brow with relief as he took in the perfect normalcy of the antique shop. 'I can quite honestly say it's going to be a long time before I wish for anything again.'

'I should bloody well hope so!' Simon exclaimed. 'I don't think any of us want to go through that again.' He rested his hands on Toby and Katie's shoulders, in an effort to subdue their excitement. They, along with Timmy, were buzzing with extradimensional enthusiasm, having witnessed the djinn being captured and released, along with going through the roller-coaster of the magick whirling around them. No doubt they would be enraptured with stories of sorcery and fancy themselves as wizards and witches after this adventure. They were already enthusiastically talking about spells and spirits, and probably only moments away from chasing each other around the store trying to cast spells of their own. 'That's enough excitement for one day, at least,' Simon said, gently reining the children back before they got too carried away.

Deirdre had lowered herself down into one of the wing-back chairs. She had originally moved backwards and away from the group to take a seat, moments before the djinn put the shop back into its rightful order. After the world had stopped spinning, the chair had been moved to the other side of the room. Whether that was where it had always been before, or was another one of the djinn's cruel jokes, Deirdre wasn't sure. She didn't much care, either. She was tired, and simply needed to rest.

'I'm getting too old for this,' she grumbled, rubbing her left knee. It had started to go stiff, standing on the perimeter of the paranormal phenomenon. 'Don't think I'd have much fancied ghost-hunting back when I was your age, either, though. I don't know how you people do it.'

Magick, investigating the occult, putting paranormal problems to rights; it all came as second-nature to Sam. Although he did enjoy the mystified way others often saw his work. He straightened his lapels, clearing his throat with an air of faux-modesty. 'It's nothing at all,' he said, although he sounded rather pleased with himself for something that was apparently nothing, 'all in a day's work.'

'Do you fancy a lift back with us, Deirdre?' Terry asked, taking the old woman's hand.

'Oh yes, thank you, Terrence, darling,' Deirdre said, allowing him to help her up. 'I'm very glad you're back. And that you're not a chicken anymore.'

'We're going to be heading home now. If, of course,' he turned and looked to Sam and Alice questioningly, 'you don't need us for anything else? Now all the furniture's been warped back into place, it seems we've one less job to do at least.'

'Yeah, I think that's everything,' Alice said, looking around. 'The djinn's gone, the shop's tidy, the world is back to normal. I don't think there's anything else?' She cast a glance back over her shoulder, and Sam confirmed with a shake of his head. 'We're all good. So please, go home, have a good night's rest. You deserve it after all of... This.'

Alice smiled warmly at them, the group of people who had just experienced the strangest, most surreal day of their lives. In the face of everything, and after all they'd been through, they had helped stop the djinn from causing more chaos. Having been a part of the ritual and witnessing the djinn depart, she hoped, would give them a sense of closure to the whole ordeal. As she looked at them, she could see the worn and exhausted expressions on their faces, their eyes betraying the fatigue which they all felt. Everything they had been through now catching up with them.

'Thank you, everyone,' she said as they all began to ready themselves to leave, 'we really couldn't have done it without you. I know it's been weird, but you've been an incredible help.'

'And thank you,' Simon said, 'both of you.' He seemed almost humbled, and decidedly more cordial than he had been when he greeted them for the second time that day. 'I was an obstinate prat earlier, but you didn't give up on me or Terry. I don't know what would've happened if you hadn't been so...' He paused, trying to think of a polite way to say "irritatingly persistent." '... Determined. I- We're all grateful for everything you've done. As unimaginably unsettling as it all was.'

'You had every right to be,' Sam said with an understanding smile. 'You reacted as any rational person would. I'm just used to living outside the realm of the rational.'

One by one, the group left the shop, expressing their gratitudes as they made their way back home to their now much more normal lives. None of them would forget the events that had transpired in a hurry, for better or for worse, but at least it was behind them now, and things had been put right again.

All except for Deirdre, that is. Although she was grateful they had listened to her story, and they had brought an end to the ordeal, not all was quite back to normal. Cedric was still in the hospital, healing after his injuries, and he still would be for a little while longer. Alice wished there was more they could have done to help him, too, but as the djinn had said: "what has been done can not be undone." Still, although she knew they'd done all they could, it didn't stop her feeling empathy for the woman and her husband, for whom the djinn's impact would still be felt for a while.

'Well, I'd say that was a bloody good day's work,' Sam said when it was only he and Alice left in the store. He rested a hand on her shoulder. 'Not bad at all for our first djinn. And you were fantastic, brewing up that spell. You wouldn't even know I was unconscious and quite concussed only a few hours ago.'

'I did what I could,' she replied, gently inching her shoulder away from his hand. The djinn's words hovered uneasily in her mind. In the time she had known him, through the strange cases and adventures they had shared, she knew Sam Hain was a good man; but there was still much about him that remained a mystery. It was part of his charm, that air of mystique, a life lived outside of the ordinary. But what the djinn had told Alice had left her feeling uncomfortable. 'Just one question,' she said.

'Hm?'

'You could have trapped him in the vase again, or destroyed him like you have other things before. After everything he's done, how did you know the djinn would simply leave peacefully if you set him free?'

Sam offered a slight smile. 'In short? I didn't,' he said, honestly. It was a gamble, but he did what had seemed right to him. 'From what I know about djinn, they're not demons. More like trickster spirits, but they can still be bargained with. They're duty-bound not to break their deals, but they're clever at finding loopholes.'

Reaching over to one of the shelves, Sam picked up the spherical astrolabe. It had been moved from the floor back to the display while the rest of the shop had warped too. Black burn marks, from where the energy had been beaming through, streaked in thin lines across the brass rings.

'You can't sell this to a collector in this state,' he said, examining the marks, and pulled out his wallet. 'Especially as it's been through the interdimensional wringer, it's probably best if I hold on to it for safe-keeping.'

Removing a few crumpled notes from his wallet, he placed the money down on the desk next to the till. He may sometimes play fast-and-loose with the accepted norms, especially when very few supernatural situations left room for normality, but he wasn't about to let an independent business be out of pocket.

'Anyway,' he continued, 'the djinn wasn't evil. Even if he did cause his fair share of chaos. I think he was a bit more like a caged animal, lashing out at his captors. If you'd been imprisoned for gods know how long, forced to obey whoever opens your cage, wouldn't you be the same?' He laughed. 'I know I probably would.'

'Yeah,' Alice said uncertainly, 'I suppose I can understand that.' She almost could understand it, although she didn't necessarily agree with it. If she had been in his shoes – not that the djinn wore shoes – she wouldn't take out her pent up anger on innocent people. She couldn't imagine enjoying causing suffering, and she wasn't comfortable with the fact that Sam seemed to suggest he would. Although maybe she was reading too much into it.

Venturing over to the window at the front of the store, Sam leaned forward and craned his neck up to look at the sky. It seemed clearer, the clouds having departed and revealing the pinky-purple of darkening twilight. The faint glimmer of stars were starting to shine in the dusky sky. 'Well, looks like the weather's cleared up,' he said casually, 'no pet precipitation. We should probably get going.'

'Sounds like a plan,' she said. Heading towards the door, she held the shop key in her hand and removed her tote bag from the coat rack. 'If you head out, I'll lock up.'

'Of course. I'll walk back with you, if you fancy? It's starting to get dark,' he said. He almost felt patronising, suggesting that he walk her home; it wasn't that late, after all, and he knew Alice was perfectly capable on her own. She had probably walked these same streets many a time before, and far later into the night. (Although one of those occasions was the incident on All Hallows' Eve, which wasn't a good scenario, but as far as he knew that wasn't exactly representative of Islington's usual nightlife). Even so, he couldn't not at least offer, especially as he didn't mind the idea of enjoying a brief evening stroll with her anyway.

Alice seemed to consider this for a brief moment, before shaking her head politely. 'Nah,' she said, 'that's quite all right, thank you. It's hardly far to go from here, and I need to pop into the supermarket on the way anyway.'

'As you wish,' Sam said with a humoured smile, 'at least that one didn't knock me out.' He adjusted his jacket, straightening his lapels as he examined himself in the antique mirror, and opened the door. 'See you again soon, though.'

'Soon,' she repeated. 'And if I find out about any more cursed or haunted items here, you'll be the first to know,' she added with a chuckle.

'I should hope so! Wouldn't want to miss the excitement,' he smiled, 'as long as you don't give me another concussion.'

'That was the djinn, not me!' she said in mock-defence. 'Although maybe it was a poor choice of phrasing on my part...'

'In any case, while I was busy nursing my blunt force trauma, that was some pretty potent witchcraft you weaved. Not bad at all given what you had to work with. I'm impressed.' He looked at Alice with a proud expression, before diverting his attention off down the alleyway. 'Anyway, I shall leave you to your grocery shopping. Have a good evening.' With that, Sam began to make his way towards the tube station.

'Thank you,' Alice called after him, 'and you too.'

Sam didn't turn around, but he raised his hand to wave behind him, calling back a courteous "thank you!" He continued walking down the alley, off and into the night, with the satisfaction of another paranormal problem resolved.

He is not what he seems, the djinn's words haunted Alice's mind as she watched Sam walking away, *that you will know soon enough*. She still didn't quite know what to make of what he said, what he could possibly have meant, but it didn't sit right with her. It could imply that Sam harboured some dark and terrible secret, a part of himself he kept hidden, or simply that he had a passion for Dungeons and Dragons and electro-swing music (not that either of these last two would be particularly surprising, she thought).

She hoped, in her unknowing, she was worrying about this more than was necessary.

Epilogue

It is hard to describe the true nature of the aethereal plane in a way that is comprehensible to the human mind. It is a dimension which exists slightly out of step with the material plane, a realm that is as ephemeral and ever-changing as the wind.

Many things exist in the aethereal plane. Ideas drift like echoes upon the winds of imagination, thoughts that float along wisping strands of the nascent dreaming. Spirits and elemental beings of the air dwell within these currents. They can exist everywhere and nowhere at once, moving about their dimension as a breeze, bestowed with both the grace of a zephyr and the strength of a hurricane.

It was a breath of quite literal fresh air for the djinn. The moment he was released from his shackles, his bonds to the vase broken, he had departed the terrestrial realm and crossed the threshold into the aethereal. It had been almost a hundred and fifty years since he had last existed in this realm outside of a physical reality, in this form of being. The feeling was beyond freeing.

While he drifted about in an unearthly state,

soaring through the boundless currents of the aether, the djinn turned his attention back towards the earthly plane. Though he still harboured much distrust and disdain for humankind, and it would take more than a singular act of kindness to change his opinion, he found his mind wandering back to those who had released him. His unwitting masters turned liberators. He could glimpse their lives from the aether, as easily as one might change the channel on a television.

Cedric had been discharged from hospital early. Only a few days after the incident in the antique shop, Deirdre received the call to say that her husband was coming home. According to the nurses, he was recovering at a remarkably rapid rate – especially for a man of his age – and that he was healing "as if by magic." Not that the djinn would know anything about this, of course; he had promised not to meddle in the affairs of humans, and it would be terribly improper if he had broken that. Although, for the sake of argument, if he had done that, he wasn't convinced that simply nudging things in the right direction was all that bad.

Deirdre had been taking care of him from the moment he returned home. At first she doted on Cedric too much, offering him every creature comfort under the sun, when all he wanted to do was rest. Then there were times when the stress would get to her, having to tend to his needs, treating his skin graft by gently washing and moisturising it, feeling more like his nurse than his wife. But, more than anything, she was just grateful that he was home, safe and well, again. Cedric seemed more attentive than usual, too, listening to Deirdre's stories about what she'd been up to while he was in hospital. He'd missed her, and while he wasn't able to do too much until his skin had fully healed, he enjoyed listening to her. He even seemed – or, at least, pretended – to care about Ingrid's new tablecloths. Deirdre was grateful. Even if she did have to patiently tolerate the football being on the television round the clock.

Next door, Simon had taken some time off from work. The event of Terry's "disappearance" already meant his clients had been referred to another lawyer with the firm, until Simon was able to resume working. Although the situation had been resolved – though few would believe the details of how – rather than picking up where he left off, Simon put in for some vacation time. He finalised the paperwork on his end and forwarded it to the firm, and decided to dedicate the next two weeks to uninterrupted family time. After fearing his husband had gone missing, he wanted to fully embrace their time together.

Terry had done the same. Even if he was back to his normal, human self again, being transformed into a chicken and back by magick beyond comprehension is not something one gets over after a good night's rest. He needed the time off for a bit of self-care. Enjoying weekends out with Simon, Toby and Katie, nights in with some decent movies, and – while the children were at school – spending some quality time with Simon, was precisely what he needed.

Timmy still wished he could fly again. He had told stories to his friends at school about the genie, and how he had been able to fly. None of them believed him, of course, as whenever anyone asked him to prove it – often requesting he demonstrate by flying – he would say that the genie had gone home. While this was true, it didn't mean he couldn't fly; just not on the terrestrial plane. Sometimes, when the boy fell asleep and his mind would drift amidst the dreaming, the djinn would show him how to fly through the realms of the aethereal plane.

Meanwhile, Alice was busy ruminating on the last words the djinn had spoken to her. His words would echo in her mind in the quiet of the evening, a thought reminding her of the ominous message, and she would think about them. And worry. She wasn't sure what the implications were, but the thoughts left her unsettled and uncertain, an unshakable feeling that something was terribly wrong. Even when she tried to push the words to the back of her mind, there they remained: a niggling doubt and distrust, gnawing at her consciousness. And a lingering sense that one day soon, she would know what they meant, and she doubted it was anything good.

The djinn had, of course, spoken truthfully. He was commanded to, after all. But he had also chosen to speak vaguely. To know too much too soon would do no favours... It wouldn't stop the events which were already in motion.

As he watched them go about their lives again,

undisturbed by his presence, he wondered if they now understood the power of words. How the things they spoke had manifest, causing harm and suffering to themselves and those around them. How little humans concerned themselves with consequence and repercussion, too focused on their own selfish and narrow views, and only when it is too late do they tend to regret their actions.

Perhaps, he thought, now they might be more careful what they wished for.

ABOUT THE AUTHOR

Bron James is an author of urban fantasy, science fiction and magical realism. He was born with a silver pen in his mouth and has been making up stories for as long as he can remember. He is probably best known as the creator of the *Sam Hain — Occult Detective* series of urban fantasy novellas.

Bron's life is largely shrouded in magick and mysticism. He presently lives in London, sharing his flat with more spiders than he can count, and a ghostly presence which likes to hide his keys. He spends his days mostly delving into the city's many secrets, writing strange stories, drinking tea, and dreaming improbable dreams.

~

www.bronjames.co.uk

REVIEWS FOR
SAM HAIN — OCCULT DETECTIVE

"Imagine *Constantine* written by Douglas Adams for *Doctor Who*, and you'll be roughly in the right area for this highly enjoyable series. Bron James skillfully weaves a thrilling tale of private detective Sam Hain and his plucky assistant Alice as they investigate murder, magic and other paranormal events."

-Jeremy Biggs, Subversive Comics

"This book rocks. Not only does it invoke that great feeling of reading a paranormal mystery with great characters and a beautifully detailed setting, it also gives you the detective story thrill. This is a series of tales connected into a peculiar narrative that was a pleasure to read."

-Ellan Lir Aldryc

"Highly recommended, a well structured read and characters who are hugely engaging and likeable. Just try to put it down, you'll happily fail!"

-M. L. Vance

SAM HAIN — OCCULT DETECTIVE VOLUME I

A collective volume of the first six stories in the *Sam Hain* series, featuring the author's preferred text and illustrations by Camilla Winquist.

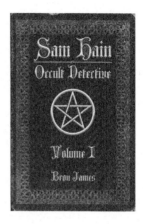

-All Hallows's Eve
-A Night in Knightsbridge
-The Grimditch Butcher
-The Regents
-The Eye of the Oracle
-Convergence

After leaving a party late one Halloween, Alice Carroll has a run-in with something she would much rather forget. Haunted by nightmares and visions, she tries to carry on with her life as normal, all the while feeling as if she is losing touch with reality. Just as her visions become too much to bear, she is helped by the enigmatic Sam Hain, a self-proclaimed occult detective and alleged aficionado of the abnormal.

Together, they embark on a series of adventures, investigating paranormal cases, cracking clandestine conspiracies, exploring the ethereal, and battling with forces far beyond the real. Meanwhile, in the abyss of some unworldly dimension, an evil is stirring, and from across the void a darkness is coming... If Alice thought her world had turned upside-down on Halloween, she hasn't seen the half of it yet.

Available on Amazon Kindle, Paperback & Hardback

Printed in Great Britain
by Amazon